Writings

On the Wall

Edited by
D.G. Sutter and Anthony Laquerre

Seven Archons
Massachusetts © 2012

Cover Sketch by Anthony Noel
Cover Illustration by Gary McCluskey
Format and Design by D.G. Sutter

ISBN-13: 978-0-9883146-0-3
Printed in the United States of America
Seven Archons

The Stories

20 % Off
Dakota Taylor

This is where my story begins: the day I was born. I was thirty nine years old. It was seven AM. My name tag read Douglas Smallwood and it was pinned next to a button of a black and yellow, smiling cartoon face. My life was pre-packaged just for me. Everything had its place. Nothing was out of order. This was the world as I knew it. Everything I owned had a barcode. Everything I broke had a warranty. Every car had a parking space. I used to be just another number, another slave to the consumerism culture and its masthead, but they say it's better to rule in hell than serve in heaven, after all.

My pre-packaged family was forever preserved in an oak framed photograph on my desk. Janet's familiar tight lipped smile and red curly hair was the only thing of her you could see. The rest of her face was ash on my desk, like my social security card. Our son, Joshua, was wearing his favorite baby blue polo. His hair was long enough to cover his eyes, but his lips were unable to cover his crooked toothy smile. Ann, our daughter, was only an infant in that picture, but her green eyes were enough to make your heart melt. The picture was taken in our backyard, the day before Joshua's seventh birthday.

Rosie, our chocolate Labrador was two years old at the time. We assumed she ran away—for whatever reason we couldn't understand—and probably got hit by a car or picked up by animal control. The next day we found out what truly happened to our family dog.

The temperature was cool for a summer day in Arizona, about one hundred and one degrees—the perfect temperature to have a few cold beers while steaks sizzled on the grill. Brian explained the advantages of having underground sprinklers while I flipped the burgers. I was genuinely interested and was about to ask about installing misters, but my head started to throb and my stomach tightened. Brian's neighborly tips became incoherent gibberish, and the only sounds I could focus on were the kids laughing and chasing each other in the yard.

I tried to recall if the children were wearing shoes to protect their feet from scorpion stings, but my thoughts changed course when I noticed the burgers and steaks. The pink hamburger meat looked like brains cooking in the skull of a death row inmate, on their personal D-Day in the electric chair. I stared at Brian's chubby face peppered with five o' clock shadow. He uttered silent words while the sound of the grill drowned out any other noises in the background. Brian doused the coals with lighter fluid and I watched in horror as the flames engulfed the steaks and racks of ribs.

Images of cows being led into the slaughterhouse flashed in my mind. Genocide, cannibalism, the only words I could find any meaning in, until my vision went black and all I heard was my own breathing. My normal perception returned as fast as it left me, and Brian said "…Peruvian Torch, San Pedro gardens in everybody's back yard but that's just me."

All of the meat on the grill was black and smoking, and when I looked over at Janet she gave me half a smile and sipped her Corona. Brian slapped me on the back. While he stared blankly at my shaking hand and the ruined food, he said in an amplified voice, "Hey, where's the birthday boy at?" before slugging off to grab another Bud Ice.

"Rosie! Look mom, it's Rosie. She came back!" Joshua said, like he had just opened his favorite birthday present.

Rosie's coat, which had once been bright and healthy, was matted and patchy. Rosie, who fit the clichés of man's best friend and loyal companion, was reduced to dingle berries clinging to her ass and bloody bite marks on her legs. This couldn't have been the same dog we played fetch with just days before. This canine looked like an abused animal from a shelter commercial—a dangerous, forgotten stray. We all watched as Joshua stared at Rosie in awe and surprise.

I yelled at the monstrosity, "Rosie!"

No reply. I yelled again and it turned its head towards me. On some instinctual level she acknowledged me, but I could see in her blue, glazed over eyes that inside, there was no life left. It was an infected shell of a mammal. Her lips peeled back, revealing sharp canines. The bastard's jaw quivered as it growled. Foam dripped from its mouth in an endless stream. Deep, bloody gashes marked the side of its face. What was left of its eye oozed yellow discharge. Most likely, a pack of rabid prairie dogs had gotten a hold of poor Rosie, probably when she was digging to hide her rubber chew toy.

It turned its head back to Joshua and without warning lunged forward, knocking his shoulder towards the ground, and biting into his neck. She latched onto Joshua's Adams apple and shook her head furiously back and forth, until it detached from his throat and a trail of purple, vein-lined cords was left lying in the brown, crusty grass. Joshua stared at the clouds while his body twitched and convulsed, blood squirting from his throat in quick spurts, dousing his face and the collar of his shirt. Brian hurled full Corona bottles at the beast, but it ignored his feeble attempts.

Joshua, who was just starting to make friends that appreciated him, was punished with a gruesome slow death. Rosie bit the end of his pants leg, continually shaking her head, and then dragged my son's body across the street into the long stretch of desert. Something about a boy dying with his dog seemed almost romantic, until I saw the trail of blood left from the horrible scene. Images flashed in my mind of Rosie tearing Joshua's arm off while vultures screeched, pecking out his eyes, filling up on leftovers. Janet's high-pitched whining sounded like something from a cheap horror movie. Brian tried to calm her while getting the paramedics on the phone.

I stood in the backyard looking stupid and holding my spatula, finally puking on myself when I made the grim connection of the Italian sausage links on the grill to Joshua's intestines.

*   *   *

After a year of counseling, Janet was still an emotional shut-in. My wife of twenty years was reduced to nothing but an emotionally devoid shell of a mammal. After Joshua's birthday we never made love again, but after six months started to have tense, rigid sex. After a while, even that ended. Conversations at the dinner table were revised to small talk of the weather and work. We no longer had cookouts, showed up to events, or connected with family at all, unless concerned relatives stopped by to check on us.

The only time Janet showed any concern for anything besides Ann was when I passed out in the bathroom after getting out of the shower. I explained to her that I drank too much red wine and slipped on a puddle. The fall left a cut on my forehead. The cut was small but deep and needed stitches. A cat scan was insisted upon to check for concussions. The MRI was insisted upon to inspect the questionable growth in my brain. The doctor explained the tumor was inoperable, but with a little chemo it would slow and I would live for at least another three months.

That was bullshit, of course. All doctors claim you'll live three months and when you live for eight months, they look like heroes. The bored x-ray tech, chewing gum, glanced at me and went back to his paperwork behind the booth. The nurse informed me that chemo wouldn't be so bad because male balding is normal at my age. The doctor said my insurance checked out and he'd like me to come in for another scan before we start talking chemo.

Therapy, conditioning, these words made no sense to me. The therapist he sent was an in-house psychiatrist, so I would only have to take an elevator ride to get from each session. His joke held no merit with me and he left the room when I only stared blankly at him.

The text I sent Janet let her know I would be working late. I'd rather lie than give her more bad news. I drove home in silence, not wanting to hear how much money I could save on a new car or another pre-packaged pop singer. Silence is what I took solace in. The plan to cry in the driveway before walking in was ruined when I noticed Brian's Range Rover parked in my spot.

The sounds of screaming orgasms could be heard even before I opened the door. Standing in the doorway, I watched as Brian's large sweaty body seizured in pleasure on top of my wife. My long time neighbor, who once gave me lawn care tips and who I shared my beer with, was reduced to a home wrecker. He was no longer my neighbor, but a throbbing member defiling my wife. He was his swollen testicles. He was his back, covered in pimples and ingrown hairs. He was these things because they were the last features I would ever again see of him. My wife bucked against him until they ruined the leather couch I worked so long to pay for.

*   *   *

The in-house therapist set the mood for his personal medical practices by lighting scented candles and having the patient lie on a Victorian-style loveseat. Doctor Sweeney also had a way of getting results almost instantly, without having to probe into your unconscious mind and have you babble over twelve sessions that set you back ten grand. No, Doctor Sweeney was a professional. For ten grand, he could have you fixed in *three* sessions.

Once you were relaxed in the candle lit office, he would ask you broad questions and let your mind wander while you described the answer. Sweeney, in his most relaxing voice, would tell you to take slow and deep breaths. While the patient inhaled through a mask connected to a nitrous oxide tank by hoses, the doctor would ask, "When was the first time you ever encountered death?"

Most people would start in on a sappy story about their gold fish dying, or opening a present on Christmas morning to find a dead puppy their parents left in the box too long. The point was to help the patient understand and cope with death. Nobody's dog or pet fish was ever HIV positive, though. Personally, I found his method to be very effective and dove straight into it when he played Mozart to a soothing volume on his record player. It was the same song my grandmother taught me to play. Her arthritis was starting to turn her fingers inward and crooked, making it impossible to play herself.

I suspect that's why she taught me how to read music. She wanted her legacy to live on through me. Requiem was the last song I played that day. When I look back on that memory, I imagine it playing on a drive-in screen in a grainy black and white film print, Mozart's Requiem the soundtrack and only sound being emitted. Seeing myself on the big screen, dressed in a little suit and tie, my navy blue dress shorts, playing piano next to my grandmother, it was cuter than a kitten drinking milk. She was ninety one years old when she had a heart attack right there next to me. When she finally died, her body went limp and her face smashed into the piano. Her septum collapsed and blood trailed from her nose out onto the keys. My eyes closed, slamming the keys and feeling the music. I didn't realize what had happened until I felt her warm blood beneath my fingers while I played the climax.

When Doctor Sweeney asked me, "When was the first time you encountered death?" I looked over at him with his legs crossed and said, "When my goldfish died."

I laughed uncontrollably at him and he only nodded his head while writing something down on his legal pad. After lighting a cigarette and calming down a little, I mentioned to Doctor Sweeney, "Did you know that Mozart died of acute rheumatic fever?"

*   *   *

Each tick of the second hand on the clock pounded in my head like a mallet hitting steel. A bead of sweat broke and rolled down the bridge of my nose while I grinded my teeth. I resorted to pulling my hair out when I found myself laughing at nothing. My job as a retail manager was terminated, but seeing as I had nowhere else to go I still show up in uniform. The walls are an off-white color and lack any decoration, due to the employment board cleaning out the office. My co-workers avoid eye contact with me when I show up, and they assume I'm already section eight.

It only took one week of being fired, due to questionable health, to make a mess of myself. The urge to put super glue on the toilet seats became impossible to obey. At the meeting last week I contemplated stabbing the new stock boy in the jaw, or simply snapping a pen in his seat and writing a letter to the CEO explaining his apathy towards the company. My dreams shattered and my mind numbed, I resorted to grabbing a shopping cart. The greeter, whose name slipped my mind, only stared at me like some lobotomy patient on an endless loop, repeating: "Welcome to Walmart, we appreciate your business."

An undeniable humming buzzed from the florescent lights, sounding like a thousand insects screaming. Someone put a Mozart CD in the overhead radio to play throughout the building and encourage customer shopping, something relaxing. My heightened senses from an oncoming migraine made Requiem sound like it was being played through speakers at a rock concert. My blue employee vest flapped behind me as I ran down the aisles, screaming like a banshee. In the toy section a little kid shoved G.I. Joes down his pocket until the front of the cart smashed his head into the shelves, knocking over stacks of board games. A small grunt escaped from the kid when I stepped on his stomach as I headed toward the hardware section. I threw air fresheners, hatchets, and seat covers into the cart in a mindless rage. I threw endless lengths of rope, power drills, and machetes in, before heading to the grocery aisle.

An elderly woman stared at the nutrition facts on a jar of rice pudding as her hip fractured from the force of the shopping cart slamming into her at full speed. A black woman in her Sunday clothes dropped a can of tuna. I assisted her by guiding my size twelve Dr. Scholl's directly into her face. She seemed to be in shock, but I kept her conscious by slapping her to keep her awake, so she could watch me tear off the lids of coffee cans and eat the dry grains by the handful. I sniffed the clothes she planned to buy before throwing them on top of her and finding a tube of Colgate, which I squirted into my mouth, mixing it with diet cola to let the foam run down my mouth.

Giving up trying to run over her face with the cart, due to her weave getting stuck in the wheel, I unsheathed a machete and swung it in rhythm to Mozart's composition being played over what sounded like the PA system. The music got louder in my head, faces blurred, and the bright lights hanging from the ceiling seemed to enshroud my entire vision.

*   *   *

The ticks from the second hand seemed overwhelming, but the NOS I was breathing in washed over me in a wave of euphoria. Zen Buddhists don't feel this good. Dr. Sweeney misunderstands me when I tell him that I saw red. I give up trying to explain myself when he asks me for the fourth time, "So you got really angry?"

Dr. Sweeney asks me how my first round of chemo went. I reply that I need a new vest for work. Sweeney's bushy eyebrows and thick glasses give him the appearance of an owl, and in the dim light this disturbs me.

"So you haven't gone to your chemotherapy yet?" He asks, void of all emotion.

When I look at Dr. Sweeney he's texting on his phone, his pen top chewed paper thin. He doesn't notice when I reach over to crank up the laughing gas as far as it will go. Almost instantly I'm back in the den, sitting at the grand piano, practicing chords. My grandmother is telling me stories about surviving the holocaust. She tells me about one of the German soldiers inviting her into the officers' barracks. She tells me that the soldier had taken a liking to her because of her strong will, that the soldier would sneak her chocolate, and every now and then let her listen to the phonogram in the barracks. The nitrous-induced dream version of my grandmother explains that hearing Mozart playing from that phonogram was the most beautiful thing she ever heard.

After she died at the piano one of the paramedics asked me, "Can you play any Jethro Tull?"

Party Crashing

Alan Wor

Outside the window, the sun sets. The sky is just beginning to turn a shade darker than clear day. She has these long red ribbons tied around her ankles, and I wonder about those. Did she wear them when she was alive, too? If so, wouldn't they drag on the ground behind her? Wouldn't they have gotten dirty and torn?

Her dress is black—appropriately—but it's also puffy, frilly, and lacy, which makes me frown and then feel bad for judging her when she can't defend herself. Her legs— a little too much of them—are powder white, slender, but short. She has red ribbons around her wrists, as well. Her nails look unpainted, but show and sparkle unnaturally in the light, some kind of gloss or something. A final ribbon, bow-tied almost comically, clings to her neck. Above that, a delicate chin and small, pink lips.

Her eyelids lay over her eyes, covered in a heavy layer of purple eye shadow, like two tiny carpets. Her light blonde hair is in pig tails and her short bangs end just where the eye shadow begins. What is the point of all this? She is supposed to look like a doll, of course, but the colors don't mesh at all. It all seems random and gaudy, thrown together by a colorblind mortician with only minimal instruction.

Just who the hell would put pink lipstick on a corpse, anyway?

My time at the casket is done.

*   *   *

Later, I'm talking to her sister and I mention the dress and the ribbons. She says the will dictated the clothing exactly, right down to the dark green high heels. Their mother had not approved. She laughs nervously. It's full of grief, high and sharp, bordering on a scream. She will try to hide this grief away, sweeping it under tight lips and a stiff neck, and cigarettes smoked from the tips of fingers, behind the convenience store dumpster before church on Sunday.

She will fail—of course—and end up hating her mother, who already hates herself. I know. Of course, I know. There are small groups of vaguely dressed mourners all around us. They are formless and black, just like the living room carpet beneath our feet, and the couch a little ways away. I feel sorry for her in her conservative black dress and flat missionary shoes, only because she is uncomfortable in them, but wears them anyway.

"It's sad when something that's together falls apart."

She doesn't understand what I mean. She says she must have forgotten who I am and then asks my name. I say I need to use the bathroom.

I find her mother next. Her hair is a clump of blond-gray wire. She is standing by the cold fireplace. It seems that the ashes were just recently cleaned out. I want to talk to her, but the sharp sting of hard liquor wafts up from the tumbler in her hand. I act like I was just walking past her instead of toward her, but she stops me. I have always hated alcoholics.

"You...one of her boyfriends?" She speaks in sharp exhales, thick with fumes.

"Yes." It's understandable that she would think this. I might fit with her daughter. My black coat is long and pools around my feet when I stand, dragging behind me when I walk.

"So, you're into all that Gothic shit?"

"Yes." Again, it's the coat. Let her think what she wants.

"It's a bunch of bullshit." She stumbles slightly, hanging onto the sleeve of my coat, which is suddenly much too hot.

"Yes," I say. I am guarding the gates of Buckingham Palace. I will stand straight and not move a muscle. She is putting more weight on my arm, slumping into it.

"Was she...happy?"

"She might've been." She misunderstands this and begins to cry. She says it wasn't her fault. She did everything she could. The blame belongs everywhere else.

"Yes," I say. "Yes."

I gently lift her off my arm and place her onto the shoulder of someone standing nearby. He seems startled in his lime green, horribly inappropriate shirt, but he is not directly related or close. So, now he'll have a story to tell and maybe he'll even make up an appropriate meaning. That's up to him.

*   *   *

Her father finds me in the kitchen by the open glass door to the brick patio, where the funeral goers gather to smoke cigarettes in the almost dusk. Though, it's winter and cold, his jacket is open and his beer-belly strains at his white shirt. His black tie falls over his gut and curves towards his belt. It has a sliming effect on the tie, making it seem longer and thinner. As I stare, I think it may lazily reach the floor at any moment.

They are divorced. There's something wrong with the way he laughs and slaps me on the back, not just that it's a little too loud or that he hits me a little too hard, either.

"Heard you talked to the wife, boy-o. Heard you made her cry. Go easy, huh? She's got a lot to deal with. Her daughters are a handful!"

He slaps me again, followed by another loud bark of a laugh. The mourners around us shift and sway uneasily, like tall trees in a wind.

Ah, he forgot.

"It's your daughter's funeral. Shouldn't you cry or something?" It sounded right in my head.

He hits me in the jaw and knocks me through the open doorway, screaming that he's going to kill me. He tells me he's going to reach down my throat, rip out my stomach, then shove it up my ass till it again comes out my throat. No wonder his drunken wife divorced him years ago.

I can see it all—the way they were, and the way they will be. No one can stop it.

"I think most of the time people don't really mean what they say."

He doesn't seem to appreciate that, though, and from nowhere he produces a short aluminum bat. His friends or his cousins or his brothers, or just the random assortment of smokers on the porch pull him back. One of them lifts me to my feet and apologizes over and over.

"Why are you sorry?"

He doesn't know.

The young man—a boy really—who helped me up, half drags and half carries me to the couch. I let him because he wants to. The brand new, black leather is too firm and smells new. The man who helped me up sits beside me. I thank him and ask if he was close to her. He says he was her boyfriend. Oh shit, my jaw hurts.

Either he hasn't heard who I'm supposed to be, or he's too polite or tired to call me out. He jabbers on about something, football or soccer maybe. He must have big lungs. It's loud and fast, unending and impossible to follow. I stop him.

"Tell me something about her, something only you know." I say.

He is shocked, but not by me. More so, I have uncovered the shock that was already in him, just under the football and soccer. His answer shocks me equally, but I'm sure I hide it better.

"She really liked biting. She really liked me to bite her when we made love."

"That's not what I meant."

"She has bite marks all over her chest," he says.

"Tell me something else."

"There is nothing else. Everybody thought she kept secrets. I never thought that was fair."

"Be honest."

"What?"

He's a well-dressed guy in his slim black suit. It is a funeral, after all. His hair gives him away, badly dyed a spray-painted black, cut and styled so it always falls over one eye. It doesn't suit him, and suddenly I'm sure he only did it for her. I almost laugh, but again feel bad when I realize it's very sad.

"I am honest," he says.

"Why was she wearing those clothes?" This look of slack shock on his face, all the muscles release except the eyebrows, which rise slightly. It can't be very convenient for him, but then, maybe some people think it's cute.

"I guess she wanted people to think she had a secret."

"It's night outside." That is a surprise. I never lose track of time.

"She didn't, though. She was so sweet and nice, and fucking wild in bed, and—"

"I need to go before you start crying, but I suggest you find her mother and tell her all of this. She will be happy to hear it."

Shock, again. I could do this all day, but I won't.

*   *   *

She told me about the skylight in the room she grew up in. She told me how the dawn looked through it and how, in the summer, she would climb up the iron ladder in the middle of her room—with sleeping bag in tow—to camp on the roof and watch the stars emerge, like tiny silver fish from the deep water of a black sea.

Yeah, right.

She broke this window three times growing up. Once she was high, once she was drunk, and once she was angry. Her father put a padlock on it when she was thirteen, after she fell through it while trying to sneak in after a night of drinking. Three bottles of red wine stolen from her mother, polished off between two young girls, ended in thirty eight stitches.

Dawn and silver fish—yeah, right.

I climb up that ladder now. The padlock is long gone. It's wide open and waiting for me.

"Took your damn time, Reaper. Didn't I say, 'As soon as it got dark...?' Didn't I?"

There she sits, in all her useless frills and bows. The red crescent moon far, far off.

"Why do you dress that way?" I ask.

"Another thing, what the fuck did you set my mom up with that bald freak for?"

"Who?"

"That guy. You know...that guy. Green shirt? Bald? You practically draped her all over him. They're making out in his car right now." Her voice is softer than one might guess and it makes me think of the color violet.

"Oh." You never can tell with people.

"Oh, that's all you have to say?"

"Well, I guess death and sex...or something." This deflates her, like shooting a blow-up clown doll in the head.

"You could put a little more energy into it, you know? I should just call you Grim."

She stands and walks to the edge of the roof. Her heels are very high and green, and the clay shingles are very slippery, but she has perfect balance these days.

"Why do you dress that way?"

"Because it looks good." No pause at all.

"Oh."

We're silent for a bit and I watch as she shatters a shingle with her heel. I watch as she views the pieces pull themselves back together. She repeats this with her back to me.

"What do you want to do now?" I ask, after the fifth time.

"Nothing."

"Anywhere you want to go?"

"No."

"Someone you want me to talk to?"

"No, okay? No." She breaks another shingle.

"Why not?" I sit with my legs hanging through the open skylight, swinging them slightly. My coat flaps around them.

"Because it's...because there's no reason to."

"Come with me then. I'll take you somewhere."

"There's no reason to do that, either." She turns back to me. She is so young. Her eyes are so wide and blue. You could say she has her whole life ahead of her, if you were trying to be funny, but her makeup is absolutely ridiculous.

"It might change something for you."

"No."

"It might."

"Fine, fine, I give up. Do whatever you want."

"Okay." I stand and offer my hand, but she ignores me as she looks down at her feet and leans back, balancing on her heels.

"You know, I used to fight with my mother, and my father. And my sister, my boyfriend, my friends, strangers on the street. You know...all those assholes."

"It's in the past now," I tell her.

"You know, I haven't felt anything, at all, in a long time. That's how I know nothing matters."

"I know." My hand is still out to her and I will have to stand that way for a long time.

*   *   *

She smiled once. Yes, and they sat on the shore in the sand, her and the boy. The sun would set on the water in front of them and rise out of the mountains and valleys behind. Yet, there, the days grew too long for her, and the nights too short. Soon after, they dressed themselves in night, and more, night flowed through a slender, stainless steel glass into them. It left the skin red and angry where it passed.

They would leave the shore to walk the streets of the city. The sea birds were gone, even the crows. Gray dust pigeons were with them. Her heels were high and square, which made it hard to walk, and the clay on her face was heavy. A homeless man wearing a necklace of twisted metal wire and a green stone over his rags— heavy with oil and dirt—told them, "You all breathe too much oxygen for the month of winter."

Not an hour later, another asked her how much she
was for an hour. She didn't take this personally, but the
night was like day to her now, and the boy didn't care for
the copper taste it left him with. He wanted to return to
the shore. She wouldn't cry, nor even scream back at
him, but would walk the streets with the pigeons and the
night. In the city, light has to travel a long way to reach
the ground.

Not days after, she would be naked and limp—
soaked at the bottom of the shower stall—and the boy
would shake her and slap her, forcing the air into her
lungs until they were full to bursting, but she would not
push it back out. In the haze of dusk, he had forgotten
how. Yes, he could have done more. Yes, of course, could
have helped her breath. He would speak to her for long
hours after this, but she would not speak back. All her
life, she lived in the time between the sun and the sun
again.

Later, she would watch them all as they wore the
mask of grief, or rather, removed the mask of the
everyday. Her mother was there, her father, sister.
Someone would spill a cheaper wine on the carpet and
someone else would get high in the bathroom, blowing
the smoke out against the screen. Another two would

fuck in the back of a coat closet, short and desperate, the boy and the sister, actually. Yet, none of this would bother her any longer. I was with her then. She danced and traveled with me, high on the wind, to the places between the stars.

We'll stay that way for a while. Then, I will leave and she'll be set to some other task, guiding another perhaps, but she'll grow tired of this, too, eventually.

Before this, long before, she stood barefoot in a yard surrounded by a tan picket fence, held together by globs of wood glue. There were some flowers in the yard, but more weeds, and more trash and dirt. She expected things there, expected them to happen. She'd been promised.

The flowers are lies, as are the weeds and the dying olive tree that grows over the cracked sidewalk, the trash. Even so, she remembers it fondly and wishes for it now, wishing for it all again. She wants to breathe too much oxygen again. One more time. A thousand more times. A million. Forever. For all time. For everything. Just to breathe again.

Your Leg Tastes Better...
Byron Alexander Campbell

...was a thing he said which, in retrospect, should have given her pause. What did he mean by better? Better than what, than before? Better than other legs he'd tasted? When had he the occasion to taste her leg, anyway? To be honest with herself, she knew exactly when and how often to boot.

Her first husband, Gary, had been limbed, which made him selfish in the bedroom. Everything about him was arm-centric. He would grope, fumble, push, tug, and reorient her until that tell-tale tightening of the grip, after which his hands would fall away, limp and evasive. For Gary, women were just an accessory to masturbation. Hell, *everything* was an accessory to masturbation for

Gary. She'd once caught him romancing a few slices of French toast. After that, she stopped bringing him breakfast in bed.

She never realized just how bad off she was until the accident. An orgasm, like love, is something you always think you're having until you have it for real. There was a lingering vagueness concerning the precise events that led to the accident. Certainly, Gary's legs shouldn't have been anywhere near the packaging machinery, but that didn't stop the phone from ringing and Gary's boss, Sylvia, sharing the news that her husband was in the hospital and his severance package would be more than generous.

How apt that term proved to be: severance package. She sometimes liked to roll the words around on her tongue, especially when she was in bed with the new husband. The meaningless sounds that came out of her took on different flavors based on the way she shaped her mouth, affecting the texture of her orgasm. The phrase "severance package" gave her a low-key, but palpitating, climax. "Amputation" was sharp and powerful, but left her sore in the morning. "Gary" felt like a rash and made her asshole pucker.

When the phone rang after Gary stuck his legs in the packaging machinery, the caller ID read "HOT POCK." Those were the first letters in the name of the product the factory manufactured. Whenever she saw "HOT POCK", she knew trouble was on the way.

In their six years of marriage, "HOT POCK" only called four times. Three of the times were a direct result of Gary's discovery that the girl who worked quality assurance made a decent, supplementary masturbation accessory. The other one, of course, was when his hips were caught in the packaging machine.

He stayed in that hospital for two months. She came to visit as often as she could and when they released him, she was told discreetly that her husband was technically intact. Like tomatoes are technically a fruit.

His legs looked like the cross-section of a pizza box. They'd been corrugated. His loins were purple and shiny, totally inert. The functional part—through which he passed water—fused to his hairless pubis, and the rest of it was gone completely. His arms were unaffected by the accident, but no longer served a purpose except to push his mass around the house. No more masturbation for arm-centric Gary.

"HOT POCK" produced an orgasm that was giddy and restless. She inherited a new lifestyle. Part of this involved driving Gary to his Wednesday night group meetings. The group was called Paraplegic, Amputee, and Disabled Support—or PADS—and Gary wouldn't have gone except it was included in his severance package, so why the hell not?

It was at PADS where she met the new husband. Unlike Gary, he was born without the use of his limbs. Therefore, he wasn't arm-centric or leg-centric. If anything, he was mouth-centric. He was what her mother would have called a charmer. As the necessary result of a process she only vaguely understood and couldn't begin to describe, he ended up performing oral sex on her in the roomy section of her minivan, referred to in advertisements as the cargo space. She was sprawled across Gary's wheelchair while the not-yet-new husband propped up between her knees, emerging from the dark clutter of the van's floor like a questing fungus. All the while, Gary was giving testimony and drinking bad lemonade with the PADS crowd.

The stranger's mouth indulging on her was a good reminder that she'd gone without sex for over a year and a half. Masturbation was non-existent in her mind, not even a possibility. It was like spoor, she decided. Gary picked it up early and nurtured it in some damp, musky area in his mind, so it had grown to envelop him. She wasn't aware of her capability to self-please, always assumed it was something boys did.

Though they never discussed the topic, it must have been the same for her new husband. She wondered what his teenage years were like. She decided he had either thought of sex constantly, or not at all.

Gary tried, unsuccessfully, to mount her a few times since leaving the hospital. She didn't really mind it. She knew other women would have been repulsed by his cauterized organs. However, if it made Gary happy to drag his body on top of her and grind his hamburger-flesh between her legs, it was the least she could do to lie there until he had exhausted himself. Compared to their sex life before the accident, she reasoned, it wasn't all that different.

After the incident in the PADS parking lot, it seemed inevitable that Gary would need to go. She considered it a private amputation. His disability and the severance package (of which she got half in the end) complicated matters legally, dragging on for fourteen months. Realistically, Gary was gone from her life the moment her genitals juddered against the emergent husband's face, which makes it sound like it was all about sex. Of course, it wasn't. There were dozens of reasons over which she could have left him. The accident didn't change any of them. At first, it looked like a sex thing to the jury, until they heard that her new lover was a man with no arms and no legs.

After hearing that, their perspective shifted. They told one another between sessions that she must be really selfless, giving up completely to that poor man. Meanwhile — not fifty feet away in the private room provided for her defense — her fancy dress was bunched up around her stomach, as she breathlessly read the titles off the hundred dollar bindings of her lawyer's legal books and the emergent husband formed potent but nonsensical words inside her. She was awarded everything she asked for, which was nothing unreasonable.

In her dreams, his stumps unfolded into shiny metal limbs, like butterfly wings drying in the sun. He became an insect, a Shiva, multi-limbed and terrible, lopping the heads off dandelions with a hiss of his segmented forelegs. A single touch and the pillows would explode into dust. The air was thick with downy feathers and seed-bearing dandelion fluff. As the white pollutants caked her nostrils, a sensation not dissimilar to a sneeze would build. She'd watch as the Shiva-husband stalked through the house, disassembling toasters and microwave ovens, reducing dinette sets to pools of bubbling ferrofluids. His erect penis preceded him from room to room.

As the filament-like fingers on the ends of his multitudinous limbs did their subtle work, her clitoris would become engorged. Without a backward glance— *swish!*—he'd decapitate it. It took a few seconds for the nub of flesh, tumbling through the soupy air, to plop onto the mattress. Usually at this time, she woke up.

Sometimes she awoke to find him fast asleep where she'd left him, cheek plastered against her sweat-soaked pelvis, drooling into her thigh. She was always mildly surprised that Gary never changed position while she slept. As though the world could refigure itself, like items in a magician's cabinet, if she pretended not to look for a minute or two.

Gary once took her to a magic show at the civic center, when he was still whole. Over drinks, afterward, her thoughts kept returning to one question: What was it like for the girl who gets sawed into thirds and then emerges whole at the end of the show? To watch her hands and feet separate from her body, to watch as the other less stunning assistants wheeled them away— beyond her line of vision—somewhere the audience could see them, but she could not. To have to bow prettily and wink at the greasy fumbling magician, as though nothing had happened. Gary chided her, made her feel dumb for not realizing that it was all a trick. As though knowing made it any less real.

The new husband's penis was surprisingly functional and well-formed. During sex it became a deep, almost brick-like red, and radiated an extraordinary amount of heat. About once a month, she would lay him out on the bed and lower herself onto this pulsing heat. She didn't move right away, instead reaching down behind her to massage his testicles. Everything was still and silent, almost like the hall of a monastery, except for her fingers on his testicles and the twitching of his erection inside her. This could go on for hours, and she only began to move when she neared orgasm. When it was over, she would sometimes have to rub his penis with the sheet until he ejaculated, wordlessly. She did it without complaint.

However, her favorite thing was leaving him marooned down there on his stomach and wrapping her legs around his strong neck, while his body flopped listlessly. Marooned was a poor choice of words. She didn't realize that her period had arrived until she was already finished. That was an "amputation" orgasm. With a pang, she remembered looking down to see the deep red blood smeared across his face, matted into his hair. Surely, he must have noticed as he worked his tongue in and out of her, but he said nothing.

After she came, she would wipe his face down with the moist towelettes she kept next to the bed, maneuver him onto his chair, and wheel him into the bathroom. Without bothering to put anything on below the waist— she could be a tease—she would lean over to fill the tub. She would then place him inside, scrub him clean, then let the water drain while she shaved his whiskers—if necessary—and applied deodorant to the bunched hairs below his shoulders. After depositing him on the toilet, she would prepare dinner, something quick and easy like a soup. Returning to the bathroom, she would wipe him, dress him, and wheel him out to the dining room. She spooned his soup for him while they watched nothing on the television. When that was finished, she brushed his teeth—it was easier just to do it at the kitchen sink—and tucked him into bed.

She wrapped her limbs around his blank body while they slept. In the morning, they did it all again, and she was generally happy with her new life.

Only once had she forgotten to feed him. Only once had she returned from a surprise reunion with some remnants of her old life to find him wallowing in a miasma of his own piss and shit, and been nearly too drunk to know how to deal with it. Only once had she brought another man home and received him up against the wall, while from the bedroom her new husband watched helplessly. Only once had she run the bath too hot and allowed his skin to burn and blister.

"Your leg tastes better..."

...was a thing he said when she had him between her legs. When she came, she would clean him and feed him and allow him to relieve himself. They had a routine and she was generally happy. She pushed herself against him, muffling his words. She was impatient this time, to come.

He suddenly twisted his head to the side, sank his teeth into her thigh—where blood welled up—spilling into his mouth and down his smooth, featureless shoulders. He guzzled at her hungrily, his four stumps pulling at the sheets, moving him nowhere.

Her mouth shaped the word "metamorphosis."

Daddy's Glad Hands
Ralph Robert Moore

"I don't understand why the fuck the pizza isn't here! What's going on?" Toby asked.

"You didn't order it, baby! You just wrote down what we wanted," his wife said, "but you didn't actually call it in yet!"

"Where the fuck is it? We ordered it an hour ago!"

"You didn't call it in, Dad!" said Chris.

"Where the fuck is it?"

Cinder, his wife, stared at Toby. "You didn't actually order it! You just wrote down what we were going to get, but you didn't actually call it in yet!"

"I ordered it an hour ago!"

"No, baby, no. You wrote down what we were going to get, but then you never actually got on the phone and ordered it!"

"But it was over an hour ago!" Toby shouted.

"But you didn't order it! You never actually called it in. Remember? We discussed what we were going to get, and you wrote the toppings down on the back of that envelope, but you never actually picked up the phone and ordered it!"

"It's been a fucking hour! What the fuck is wrong with them?"

"Dad, you have to call it in!"

"You didn't call it in, baby. You wrote down what we wanted, but you never called the pizza place, Toby."

Toby ran his veined hands through his orange, grey, and white hair.

"It's been a fucking hour!" He rolled his blue and red eyes at the black microwave oven, at its digital clock's pulsing green colon. "Fucking hour! Where is it?"

"You never actually ordered it, baby! You only wrote down what we wanted! You never actually picked up the phone and placed the order."

"What?" Toby asked.

"We decided on the toppings, but you never actually picked up the phone and ordered the pizza. We started talking, and you never actually got around to actually ordering the pizza."

"I didn't order the pizza?"

"No, *you didn't*! We discussed what we were going to get, and *you wrote* down the toppings, but you *never* actually picked up the phone and ordered it."

Toby looked down at the back of the envelope, the overlaying triangle of yellow whiteness against the rectangular white, the black ink sliding across the flap: black olives, sausage, pepperoni, mushrooms, his phone number, his address, and his name. "It's been a fucking hour. You're saying this is my fault? What the fuck…what is this? What's going on? Where am I?"

"We didn't actually order it! We discussed it, decided what we would get, but then you never actually called it in!"

Toby looked from where he sat at his place at the kitchen table, out past the wide square doorway of the kitchen, out across the shadowy white carpet of the living room, to the distant, silent front door. "Didn't we?"

"No! We never did!"

"We never…I never ordered it, actually?"

"*No!*"

"Oh. Well, what time is it now?"

"Almost two AM."

"Well, they probably don't deliver this late."

"Probably not," Cinder said.

"They probably stop delivering around midnight or so."

"Probably."

"It's probably too late for us to order a pizza tonight," said Toby.

"Probably."

"Is that okay?"

"We could just eat what we have."

"So…I just want to get this straight in my mind. There's no pizza coming?"

"No. We wrote down what we wanted, but we never ordered it. We talked about the toppings we wanted, and you wrote the toppings down, on the back of that envelope, but then we never actually picked up the phone and placed an order with them."

"So we're not having pizza tonight?"

"No. We never actually ordered a pizza. We only discussed what we would order. We never actually picked up a phone and placed an order. We never actually called a pizza place and said, 'This is what we would like to order'".

"So we never actually ordered it?"

"Right."

"So, we have to eat what we have at hand?"

"Right," said Cinder.

"Because there's no pizza coming?"

"Exactly. We never actually ordered the pizza. We discussed it, but we never actually picked up the phone and placed an order with the restaurant that delivers pizza to your home."

"So it's not coming."

"Right."

"So we have to eat what we have here in the house."

"Yeah. We could, like, there's a whole package of bologna. I could fry it up and we could have fried bologna sandwiches, with mustard."

"In a way, I think that's even better than pizza. At least at this point," said Toby.

"Okay, so do you want me to do that?"

"Have the fried bologna sandwiches, instead of the pizza?"

"Yeah. Chris, is that okay with you?"

"Sure, Mom," their son said.

"Toby?"

"Well, we're not having pizza, right? They're not going to deliver it? It's too late?"

"Right."

"And you're saying let's have fried bologna sandwiches instead, with mustard?"

"Right," said Cinder.

"Well, that'd be okay with me."

"It would?"

"Yeah. Now, what happens if they deliver the pizza just as we're about to sit down to the fried bologna sandwiches?"

"Well, what do you think we should do?"

"In a way, I think I would prefer the fried bologna. That's the way this evening turned out. Fuck it. Fuck them."

"So should we like, ignore the doorbell if it rings?" asked Cinder.

"Yeah. Yeah, we should. I mean, c'mon…fuck 'em. It's what, after midnight already? Again?"

*   *   *

Black rings overlapped each other in the skillet, creating eights where round bologna slices had puckered, popped, sweated. Nicotine filled the air, giving the kitchen a peanut butter smell.

At the kitchen table, the filter-less cigarette in Toby's limp right hand dribbled orange smoke down across the grain of the table, curling around the cold curve of his glass, spiraling upwards around the ice and wood-colored whiskey inside. Smoke tendrils rose off the iced rim, raising vertically up the front of his face, past his cheeks' angularity and piercing blue eyes. His face—even at sixty six—was peach and black, sharp-edged with elegantly wide black eyebrows. Nose length, smooth burst-vein cheeks made other men's faces look plain. Behind him—on the long glossy counter below the white mini-blinded window—a white and pink birthday cake sat off-center, topped with a wavy plastic number thirty three, unlit.

Eleven year-old Chris sat on his hands at his kitchen table seat, staring blue-eyed at his father, curled black lock hanging down across his tall forehead.

Toby rolled his head back on his neck, puffing smoke upwards, the grey exhalation bouncing softly off the ceiling, scudding across the high, black-rimmed wall clock. Three o'clock.

Cinder ducked her head, rolling her eyes under her wrinkled forehead at the uncut cake. "That bologna was even better than a pizza."

"Someday we'll eat a lot better than bologna. We still have pistachio ice cream for dessert."

"Oh, I know." She put a hand on top of his—two wedding bands, around bony fingers, golden, apart, and expensive. "I bought blue napkin rings today."

"Someday we're gonna go on a river, right Dad?"

"Damn right. We'll get on a riverboat—the three of us—and ride down the river to a gaily-lit restaurant on its shore. We'll eat oysters and fresh river fish, and have cherries jubilee for dessert."

"And you'll leave a big tip on the table."

"And then we'll ride back upstream, standing at the rail, listening to a college kid in a black tuxedo play Beethoven's Waldstein, looking at the mansions we pass set-up off the bank."

Cinder ducked her head. "I always wanted to ride on a riverboat." She rolled her eyes. "I'll need a dress."

"You'll have the finest white dress ever made, light and billowy, with white lingerie sewn in Paris."

"Toby, not in front of Chris."

"I don't mind," Chris said.

"The boy has to learn. If you care about someone, you tell them about the world."

"Mom, you'd look real pretty in a white dress. You have dark hair."

"I'd have to lose a little weight first. I know that."

"That's fine. They make dresses in all sizes. Once I saw a white dress as big as a bus, with huge ruffles halfway down and a little black hole in back for the exhaust pipe," said Chris.

"Chris, it's gettin' late," Toby said.

"Can I stay up a little longer?"

"Nope, time to get tucked in."

"Aren't you sleepy, sweetheart?" asked Cinder

"Not that much."

"The bags under your eyes are purple again. Let's go," said Toby.

Chris drew his feet up onto his chair, as if something were running around on the kitchen floor. His pure profile, his perfect nose and dark liquid eyes, his wide dark lips, his youth and promise, swiveled around from floor to father.

"Dad, can I just stay up until I'm sleepier? I know they're in there, whispering in the walls, waiting for me. If we go in too early I see their toes sticking out of the electric wall sockets."

"You can't hide from them, Chris. They rest on the ceiling and slide down the walls once your breathing becomes regular. That's inevitable. Don't try to fight the inevitable. I know. I tried. I failed."

Toby took another long, cold swallow of his whiskey, head rolling back away from its ugly neck, overly-stylish hair under the ceiling light, banding in orange, grey, and white. His unbuttoned white shirt showed the boniness of his chest, his sagging nipples, and his red, grey, and white chest hairs.

"Toby, maybe we should speak to a doctor or the government or something. He's losing a lot of school."

"That wouldn't do. Half of them are in on it, anyway. The world is controlled by puppets. It has been for centuries. The days when people like you and me would sit under an apple tree, wearing white and reading poetry to each other, are gone forever. Dog-sized, hybrid insects decide our lives now."

"Sometimes they scare me so much, though, Dad. I can't keep my eyes shut."

"Always. Fucking always keep your eyes shut."

"*Toby!*" Cinder yelled.

"I'm protecting him! Never open your eyes. Always pretend you're asleep. Let it happen. It happens, they slide back up the walls. That's it. The sun comes back up. You walk out here and your mom's fixing breakfast. Always keep your eyes shut. Focus on the bacon and eggs."

"Why don't they go after you or mom? Why do they always go after me?"

"They prefer children."

"Why?"

Toby made a helpless upper body gesture, face wrinkles and forearm muscle cords. "I don't know."

"The other kids at school, they don't have aliens going after them once the lights are out."

"Chris, they may not even know about it. It may be happening to them, too, but they may be blocking it. They may be too ashamed. It may not even dawn on them until thirty years later, when they're standing in front of a urinal in an airport terminal and suddenly—*whoom!*—there it is, pee spraying all over their pants. And you still have to wash your hands and get out of there, and catch a flight"

"Well, I wanna block it, too!" Chris's small perfect face—a copy of Toby's but smoother, much softer—crumpled around the eyes, the child angles, clenched on the skull where the wrinkles will be forty years from now. "I don't want this to be happening to me! I don't want them putting their multiple knees on my bed!"

"I know it's hard. I know. I'll protect you until you're asleep, and they finish conducting their experiments and leave. Let's go."

Chris switched his large blue eyes to his mom, pleading with a look that worked for staying up late, laying on the carpet on his stomach, blue-jeaned legs spread in front of the TV.

Cinder put her fingertips in the ashtray, like it was a fingerbowl, blackening and graying her fingerprints. She swung her eyes at her unlit birthday cake, sitting store-bought, pink and white, still and unlit, uncut behind her husband Toby. Ducking her head and peering under her eyelashes at Toby, she patted the swirled crown of her baby's head—here but gone forever, all that electricity underneath.

"That's how it is. That's it. That's how it is," she said.

*   *   *

Toby led Chris, hand-in-hand, into the boy's bedroom. It was a great green wallpapered room, half occupied by the bed, the rest by the yellow moons in the window squares. The bed was higher off the floor than usual, under an extravagantly plump coral and crimson canopy. Broad flounces and flourishes draped down the bed, making it its own room-within-a-room. Relaxing across the white oblong of the bed lay an impossibly puffy, yard-high pink comforter, embroidered with rabbits, cows, bears, kittens, and mice.

Chris turned his back on his father—slipping down his blue school clothes, small bare body ripe as smooth suffused mozzarella cheese—and pulled up his striped green and white pajamas with a little boy's head-bent pride in mastery of waistbands and buttons. Toby turned away modestly from the strip-down and pull-up.

Once Chris was under the huge pink comforter, almost half as high his father, Toby sat on the edge. A father's hand on a son's slim, striped shoulder.

"Your mom and I had been having sex for about a year when she stopped bleeding. She went to a clinic, a dirty place with plywood sign-in counters and orange fake leather sofas, where you waited for hours until they called you by a three-digit number. The following week in an 'office' the size of a closet with opened doors on both sides, anonymous people passing by in corduroy pants, they told her she was pregnant. I still remember her giving me the news in our kitchen. We cried and made out our wills.

"I was living with her then, so I could see the changes every day. It got harder and harder for her to get out of bed, the weight distribution was all wrong, and more and more when she did leave the bed in the morning, it was to throw up near the toilet. I feared for her. I really did. Everything I loved about her—the fresh milk in her face, the swing in her breasts, the belly-buttoned breathing of her stomach—went away. She got swollen. She got a pregnancy mask like she was Italian or Arabic, with hair on her arms that spread to her legs, circles under her eyes, moustache on her lips. Her belly got bigger than her breasts, then bigger than anything on her, stretching sideways and frontwards until her pores were huge, and streaky white stretch marks scarred her abdomen. Her teeth started to go, because you were sucking the nutrients out of her. Do you know what that's like, to lose three of your teeth forever, to have to eat a sandwich lopsidedly for the rest of your life?

"It got worse and worse, and then you were born. She was in horrible agony, hour after hour, getting hairier and hairier. Her big, ugly body, sunken-eyed face, thinning hair, looked like it was covered in Vaseline, the worst sort of dark Vaseline, like what's wiped off after homosexuals finish anal intercourse. Then, this veiny red tumor sagged out between her legs, swelling as big as a fist, a basketball, a watermelon, and the maternity doctor kept pinching and pinching the white tip of it, kept pinching and pinching it, and finally he popped it, and you burst out of the blood and pus, wet mouth toothlessly whining, red hands opening and clenching around air.

"We had to take you home. We were responsible for this happening to her. At the time, she mostly needed relaxation to recover, to get the flush back, the giggle, the girlish curves, the wiggle in the walk, which never did come back. You started crying and crying, hour after hour from where we caged you. We tried to help you. We let you in our bed some nights, only to see you crawl across her while she was trying desperately to recover, flat on her back, you heading towards her cracked, super-sensitive nipples to suck on them, even then.

"We placed you on your stomach every night in your crib, hoping you would die from sudden infant death syndrome so we could go back to our happy days of picnics and fucking on the kitchen floor with her back rammed against the stove or dishwasher, but there you'd be each morning, lying on your fat back, fingers and toes in the air wriggling for a tickle under the cartoon-character mobile we bought four months into Cinder's pregnancy.

"Bad as it was then, we didn't anticipate you walking. Once you started that, you could get upright, waving your pudgy arms for baby balance, and jerk forward foot-to-foot, to no matter where we were. The end of fucking, that's what that meant. Then, the end of arguing, too, because you would bawl when you tight-roped into a room and saw me backing your mom into a corner during a shirt-off, voice-up argument.

"But then—about the time you turned seven—I started noticing how nice your skin was. I mean it really was, and still is, though I know that won't last. Look at me. But seeing you lying on your stomach on the living room floor in front of the noisy, blue glow of the TV, like any dad I started noticing how smoothly your skin stretched over the bones of your arms and legs, and once—when you lay down to watch TV without a top on—I saw the perfect absence of pores on your back, something kicked in.

"Because that's all it is, it's skin. We build cathedrals, stand on top of the green grassy hill and put helmets on our heads while horses gallop down the slope, bend over illuminated manuscripts with ruby and charcoal on our white fingertips, tap animated gifs in HTML, stand behind the white van marked in block letters *Fresh Fish*, unloading dead bodies instead, the weight of head wobbles and stiff limbs passed hand to hand, all of it for skin.

"So here we are, and what am I supposed to do, me with a destroyed wife? Is that skin, that sensuality, infectious? Let me tell you something—father to son. In this world, there are terrible mysteries and hints that caress us, ghostly fingertips under our chin. Sometimes, the best gift in this world is ignorance. God never showers His kindness more on us, than when He allows us to forget."

Toby swiveled his carefully coifed head. "Uh-oh, I just heard the insectile antennae-tapping slide down the inside of the walls, towards the sockets. I think their three-fingered hands are starting to reach out, reach out towards you."

Chris shivered, just a child.

Toby pulled out a text.

"In the great, green room there was a telephone and a quiet old lady, whispering hush."

"…and a quiet old lady whispering hush," Chris repeated.

"Goodnight, Mom. Goodnight, clocks. Goodnight, stars. Goodnight, air. Goodnight, noises everywhere."

"Goodnight, Mom. Goodnight, air. Goodnight, noises everywhere."

"Goodnight, faith. Goodnight, hope. Goodnight, young bodies that smell like soap."

"Goodnight faith. Goodnight hope. Goodnight the power of soap."

"Here we go, just like before. Here we go, behind a closed door."

"Here we go, behind a closed door."

"I'm not a gem. I'm not hard and crystallized that way. I do what I want to. What the hey?"

"What the hey?"

"Here they come. Here come the aliens. Tell me, what do you think of as you fall asleep?" Toby asked his son.

"I pray for you. I pray for Mommy. I think of the wonder on the waiter's face."

Chris shut his eyes double-tight—a poor, innocent child chosen for this, face so much like Toby's, but fifty-five years younger.

You had to admire his courage. You had to think, each time. Toby looked down at his son underneath his yard-high coverlet. "Here they come."

His left hand draped down, immediately seized by Chris's clawing fingers. "Here they come."

Toby raised his right hand, left hand weighted down by the grasp of Chris's fear. As he held his son's squeezing terror in his left hand, feeling it jump and clench, Toby's right hand rose in the air. Toby's piercing blue eyes watched once again as the index finger of his own hand glued against his thumb, middle finger stood out, ring finger and pinky glued against each other, until his right hand had but three fingers—not an easy thing to do—left hand still held in the painful squeeze of his son's fear. The three-fingered right hand slipped under the yard-high covers, slipped onto that smooth, suffused mozzarella cheese—such a dirty, dirty little brain rolling round in a car trunk—and when Chris's lower limbs, once again touched, surprised, threatened, invaded, stiffened, Toby said in his hoarse whiskey voice, "Don't worry, little one…"

The hand glided upwards. "…don't worry, my dear. Daddy's here."

The Break-Up
Dave Fragments

A few years ago, when I knocked on the inside of my front door to call Zipper, my greyhound, to his nightly romp, the door knocked back. I was certain that I'd heard two distinctly feeble knocks through the approaching thunder of paws. When I opened the door Dirk, a drinking buddy, lay in a crumpled heap on the porch. Zipper—being more speed than nose, more bladder than brains—vaulted Dirk "en passant", and disappeared into the darkness to chase the rabbits and squirrels.

"Hey, buddy, your dog just stepped on me four times," Dirk slurred.

"Why are you laying on my porch?" I asked, not knowing what to make of the man.

He laid fallen-down, disgusting drunk, blotto, blitzed, and oozing. His clothes were soaking in a puddle of his own spew, reeking of feces and urine, and seeping into my porch. He'd never crashed on my porch before that night. I mean, I'd seen him out-and-out wasted, doing a pub-crawl before, but never like that and I never imagined he would use my house as a crash pad.

"You're a crapulent mess! How dare you pass out on my porch."

"My birthday celebration is officially over."

"Your birthday was Tuesday. It's Thursday night."

"Hell'uva birthday party and pub crawl, huh? I might be getting older but I ain't lost the stamina." His voice trailed off into spasms of hacking, gagging, and groaning. "Can I crash on your couch, bro? We got stuff to talk about, serious stuff. Girlfriend talk."

I hesitated to step towards him without HAZMAT gear. Well, to not exaggerate the story, not a full-body HAZMAT spacesuit, just latex gloves and tongs. I avoided his unwanted fluids, as the vile liquids oozed across my porch. That stuff eats waterproof varnish, you know.

"You didn't even invite me for a piece of cake, let alone a pub crawl. Get on the gravel. I'm going to hose you down."

"But, bro, it's cold out here."

"But, bro, my ass. The bromance is over. If I'm not good enough to party with you, then you're not clean enough to pass out on my furniture, at least not like that. The best steam cleaner in the world couldn't get your stain out of my upholstery. It's the hose or the driveway," I insisted.

Dirk closed his eyes and tried to fall asleep. His lids stayed closed for about fifteen seconds, before he cursed the wood.

"I thought about you, but I lost my cellphone in the folds of Leila over at Murphy's Dew Drop Inn. I didn't want to forget you, but then, circumstances…can I come inside? I wrecked my car on…'bout a block that way." Dirk pointed indiscriminately in three directions. "Call the fuzzy-wuzzy cops for me. I'm so wasted."

Don't get me wrong, I felt bad about snapping at him and treating him like a filthy pig, but steam cleaning costs more than hose water, and beige fabric shows bodily fluid stains forever. My second ex-wife taught me that. Even my dog has more sense than to frolic in the mud and try to come into the house.

I phoned the police and reported the wreck, while Dirk crawled onto the gravel driveway. He peeled off his precious Joe Hardy t-shirt, which he paid too much for, and dropped his designer jeans to reveal faded and holey jockeys. All hat and no cattle. I wondered if he would ask his dry cleaner to restore his fancy duds or throw them out, and then I realized that I didn't care if he was fashionably dressed, naked, or wearing a tutu. Sackcloth and ashes might've been appropriate, but that was too biblical to say out loud. I merely squirted him with the cold water and aimed the hose for maximum shrinkage. He squealed like a little girl. The water cleansed a two-day binge crud from his bare body.

"I found this gal dancing near in a flimsy whimsy at the Purple Pussy."

"Dude, that's a real dive for crack whores and sewer sluts."

"But she had these humongous ta-tas, soft ass, deep hole. She gave me that new aphrodisiac drug and turned me into a raging nymphomaniac, just like her. Nonstop, never-ending screwing, beyond anything you can imagine, eight, nine times—non-stop all night. She's

God's gift to man-sluts of all ages, the once in a lifetime nympho. She called me her best man-whore ever, in all her life, never to be surpassed."

"Better than the Crisby twins?"

"The Crisby twins were dogs by comparison."

That wasn't nice of him. My first wife was one of the Crisby twins. I almost shoved the hose down his throat, but instead I dowsed him a second time with the spray. I especially hit the red hickeys on his torso and his private parts with the cold water. He deserved a little bit of rough treatment for acting like a crazed beast in rut. I waited for his body to turn bluish and for him to rattle his teeth, before I let him brush the water from his body with his trembling hands.

"You can't step into your mess on the porch. I will not have your filthy footprints on my carpets."

"When did you start to care so much for rugs? I thought we had a bond, like brothers."

"It's over, my dear."

I hosed his mess from the porch and pointed to the clean spot. "Stand right there and don't move until I get a towel. You act like an animal. You degrade yourself like a cheap monkey at the zoo, and then you want sympathy. You ain't getting it from me."

He must've heard the scorn in my voice and seen it in my face. He blushed.

"Don't be so judgmental."

"*Ha!*" I yelled from the hall closet. I threw him a ragged towel, and he rubbed his shaking body dry and wrapped the towel around his waist. I wrapped the hose around its holder.

"You shouldn't be so mean to me," he sobbed and whimpered. "She's coming for you tomorrow. She said she needed a day to recover."

I thought my ears were hallucinating what they'd heard. I stopped and stared at him, unsure of what he meant. "Who will be mine tomorrow?" I asked.

"That girl you've been dating—Amy or Alma—sumthin' beginning with an A...Abigail?"

"Amelia? My Amelia? What about her?"

"She, she...she's the one." He shivered.

We stood silently for a good ten seconds. In such a matter of the heart, I wanted no chance of misunderstanding. I wanted to know for sure that he accused my Amelia of being his slut. "She's the one, what?" I asked.

"She's the one I met at the Purple Pussy, who stole my wallet and bought the new aphrodisiac, and I spent two days giving her my personal DNA injections. Oh, God in heaven, she told me not to tell you about that. I'm a jerk, a real jerk," he said in one breath. He smacked his forehead with his fist, twice.

"Are you sure?" I asked.

"Oh yeah, I'm sure. The Cherbourg umbrella tattoo hides in her Brazilian, just like yours." He gave me one of those sad-sack puppy-dog-eye looks, pleading for a pat on the head, a bowl of food and a warm bed for the night.

Instead, I beat the crap out of him, punched him silly, blackened his lights, and kicked him in the balls a few times. Then, I dragged him onto the porch swing and covered him with the canvas cover for the gas grill. A couple of hours later—when he sobered up—I beat him again, because the first time felt so good. Zipper approved with a wag of his tail. I gave Zipper the steak I would have fed to Dirk if, and only if...

When he woke again I had the police take him away. I waited until lunch to text Amelia that it was over and to never speak to me again, even un-friended her on the Internet. Two weeks after, the local newspaper reported that Dirk married Amelia. They divorced a year later. I wish them all of the happiness they gave me. Each year on the anniversary of their divorce, I send both of them a single dead rose, wrapped in a black ribbon. I never get a thank you note from either of the unhappy couple. Gee, I wonder why not. It's such a fitting gift to celebrate a break-up, don't you think?

Ghosts
Eric Pollarine

The first time I got high off a ghost, I didn't really know I was getting high off a ghost, because I was drunk and running crushed Ritalin up my nose at three and four tabs a time. Let me tell you something of running crushed Ritalin up your nose. You think Coke is bad for your sinuses? Well, then fuck you, 'cause you ain't never done Ritalin. Don't settle for generic Ritalin, negative. I had a generic script for Ritalin once and I can tell you with absolute certainty, that you will not enjoy it.

Ritalin works one of two ways. The first being that you're naturally hyper, I mean really hyper and it slows you down. The second being that you're naturally normal, and when I say normal, obviously I mean really normal, not blowing lines of Ritalin and drinking Thunderbird because it only costs two dollars, then you go up. That's how I got it. I was normal, but they thought I wasn't. Now I've got me a lifelong prescription to Ritalin, 'cause I'm A.D.H.D. or A.D.D. or F.U.C.K.E.D., whatever way you want to look at it.

Me, I'm an optimist—glass half full kind of guy—so I got a couple of good deals in life. Ritalin was the first. Disability due to my Service is a second. I also got scripts for P.T.S.D., and several other acronyms. I thought I was done with acronyms when I left the service, but it seems that humanity loves a good acronym.

When the convoy I was rolling with got hit by an I.E.D. (see, more acronyms) I got mangled. Shrapnel went through my leg and arms, not my body—I had armor, I was lucky. The guy next to me, aptly named "Lucky", had his face torn off. It looked like a rubber Halloween mask in the middle of the spooky isle of a dirty convenient store, fake. I looked over at his body, in the confusion and deafening high pitched sine wave drone of the moment, and he was talking to me, blabbering on and on about how he sees ghosts and how he can see his family. I tried to tell him I could see the muscles of his face moving, making words, but he died, and maybe that was the first time I ever saw a ghost. It was probably the adrenaline running through my body.

I woke up in a medevac helicopter, then passed out again, then woke up in a medical station, then out again and finally when it was all said and done...America. I think we may have had a stopover in Germany, but they were pumping me so full of morphine that it didn't matter. I had some treatments, I had some physical therapy. I had some counseling and then I had some guy discharge me, because I got crab hands now and "You can't serve Uncle Sam with crab hands," or that's what the Sergeant told me.

So, I get disability through the V.A., and from S.S.I. I had some savings from my time served, and don't have a family to take care of, so all the money is mine. I hate family, I hate the word family, and I hate the idea of family. Who the fuck needs them? All they want to do is control. Family is an act of submission. I know what you're thinking: the military is the same way, right? You're wrong. Military is water spilling out as blood, family is blood spilling out as water, that's the only way I can describe it.

I get more money now than I made in the service, and I have no responsibilities. I also have a prescription for

Ritalin and about a case and a half of Thunderbird, and also get high off ghosts.

I see them everywhere. I don't need the Ritalin or the Thunderbird to see them, but it helps to take the edge off when I do. It's a hard thing to hobble out your door and see ghosts, hard to get up in the morning knowing that everywhere you look you'll see the dead, the ethereal waves of souls crossing your path. They try to talk to me, but I cancel them out. I ain't trying to learn secrets from beyond the grave. I'm trying to figure out how much I'm going to need for the bus. I tell them to go away, but I do it with my mind. I tell them in my head. I don't want the other people to see me talking to ghosts. They wouldn't get it.

This brings me back to the first time I got high off a ghost. I was—like I said—bumping lines of Ritalin and half way through my second bottle of Thunderbird. I was on the cement slab I call a porch, just outside the apartment that is completely paid for by the government. First, I was sitting by myself, and then all of a sudden there was a man in a suit, trying to talk to me about what it's like on the other side. I looked at him and I knew right out that he was a ghost. He was a drifter. Those are the ghosts that don't have a set location. They—for the lack of a better term—drift from place to place, looking for someone to talk to, looking for a place to haunt.

I fell right out of the plastic chair and lost the rest of the crushed Ritalin to the winds, afterwards calling it a sacrifice because I started to believe in nature as God. There are no atheists in fox holes, nor any with crab hands. I'm not going to believe in old grey beard and son, or their extended family of mafia enforcers they call saints, but I'm not going to tempt nature either. I worship her. I also worship the sun and moon, because they could destroy us at any time, they just choose not to. That is more powerful than a man dying on a tree. It's immediate, like an I.E.D.

This ghost and I got on alright, but then he vanished. He walked off into the parking lot and just vanished. He had a suit and tie, he had a face, and he had a way about him that seemed dead, all dead. That's when it hit me. I was high, but it wasn't from anything synthetic, it was from that ghost. Talking to that ghost opened up my mind to the possibility that nature is a God, to the Sun and the moon, to the high I could get from ghosts (obviously, on that last one). I made it a point to see as many ghosts as I possibly could after that. I wasn't ready to talk to them, yet.

I wondered if there were any more people like me out there. So, I picked myself up off the ground and crooked-walked back into my apartment, flipped on my Google box—they own everything, Google that is—and started searching. There was a convention happening soon, a paranormal investigators convention, an unexplained phenomenon gathering. I decided to go to the portable phantom lovers Mecca when it strolled through, but it wasn't for a month. I needed something else in between to keep me going. I started to watch paranormal investigator shows, all of them. They're all fakes, shills, money collectors, and tax men. Soon, I will throw them out of my temple.

I am writing a book on ghosts. When I get it finished I will sell it, people will read it, and even more people will come to understand that ghosts are everywhere and that you can see them and even talk to them if you want. You just have to be open and ready to receive the message.

That very same day, I went to the library and took out a metric ton of books on ghosts. I didn't bump into very many on my way there or back, just a handful or so. They wanted to check out books, but couldn't. They're ghosts, and therefore by the laws of God—Mother Nature— can't. You have to have rules, even in the other plains. I kept my mouth shut, but stared at them as they tried to talk to the librarians, tried to get their attention and get their books. It's a pity that apparently nobody thinks that ghosts should read.

I came back home that first day, straight off the bus and saw the suited ghost again, this time it was getting dark, he seemed to glow. He was going to haunt someplace in the complex next to mine, but something had happened to him. His disposition was all off, less friendly. I wasn't about to speak to him (I didn't want him haunting me), but I could tell that whoever, or whatever, family he was going to haunt was in for a night they wouldn't forget. That's when it hit me: I needed to devise a strategy on how to ward off ghosts, keep 'em from getting into my place, keep 'em from haunting me like they do everyone else.

I had my service pistol, but would a ghost even be afraid of a gun? It would if it remembered what it was like to be scared of violence in life. I brought it out of its safe, my crab hands don't work as well as my old hands did, but I managed to clean it and work out a way to hold it and even fire it, if need be, but only to scare the ghosts. I'd still use it if I had to, though.

Then, I read a report on my Google box that said R.F.I.D. tags could emit low wave E.M.F. fields, which would attract ghosts, they feed off E.M.F. I took out all my books and my television, my hardware, except my Google box and printer—I need them for information—and took everything apart. I smashed anything that looked like an R.F.I.D. I made charms from QR codes on my Google box and printed them out. I made charms of words, words that would have power, like "GO AWAY GHOSTS" or "THERE'S NOBODY TO HAUNT HERE".

They were statements, really, commanding them to stay away. I got the idea from the Google box when I stumbled onto some sites about summoning spirits. Like a twenty-first century magician, I stapled sigils and signs onto my walls and doorways, and even printed out a huge QR code in several pieces, taped it together and used it as my alter rug. I bumped five crushed Ritalin and drank two more bottles of Thunderbird. It made the ghost noises go away. It seems my apartment complex is full of ghosts banging around at night.

I woke up the next day and threw out the entire cache of smashed tech. I saw the suited ghost again that morning. I was fuzzy, maybe five lines was too many. He smiled kindly at me and again tried to talk to me. This time I smiled back at him, but didn't say anything. We got along alright this way, why wreck it?

I went back inside and put my pistol in the small of my back—I needed protection just in case. I had made a few charms from the QR codes the night before, made them out of paper and rubber bands that I cut up and placed around my neck. I needed to try and keep the ghosts from coming into my body, because I read on the Google box that ghosts could possess you. I took the bus into town to see my legal dealer. I was out of Ritalin and I needed something to eat, but didn't know I would wind up a revolutionary. I didn't know revolutions could begin in Denny's. When it comes to ghosts I'm always learning.

*   *   *

I took the bus down to the drug store and a few more ghosts looked at me, but they didn't look long because I had the sigils to keep them away. The other people on the bus were capturing the QR codes with their handhelds, and I wondered if they could see the ghosts, as well, wondered if they just saw the resulting commands. After I got out and made my way into the drug store, I dropped off my prescription and then wandered around while waiting.

I turned down the magazine isle and there was the suited ghost. He didn't see me right off, but I saw him. I began to wonder if he was following me, wondered if he would begin to haunt me, like he seemed to haunt the family in the neighboring complex. He looked over at me and smiled. I smiled back. I wanted to say something to him, but didn't want to wreck the good thing we had, also didn't want him thinking it was all right to follow me around. I presented him with one of my sigils and he took a few steps back.

I backed my way out of the isle and walked towards the pharmacy. On the way, I noticed that everything had an R.F.I.D. attached to it, the whole place pumping E.M.F. This whole place was made to generate ghosts. I had to escape. This wasn't a drug store anymore. It was a hot house full of ghosts. The more I looked, the more I saw, more suits and more ties, some of them were even in civilian attire. I could feel my blood pulling through my veins, could hear my heart beating in my ears. This was a trap. This was the convoy all over again, except it wasn't a Baghdad market, it was right in the middle of a ghost market.

The ghosts were making noise, it was so loud in there, the moans and cries, the wailing of the dead, it began to make me uneasy and I reached into the small of my back. The molded plastic and carbon, fiber composite handle of the pistol made me feel better. I couldn't pull it, not here. I needed to get some Ritalin in me, some Thunderbird, ride the fucking lightening. Food was also on the agenda, needed to pad the ulcers. It's tough to keep yourself full on a diet of liquor and pills.

I jumped a little when they called my name over the P.A. speakers. I thought it might be a ghost voice. I made my crooked way back to the counter, paid the man, and took the bag to the public bathroom, where I jabbed three pills into my mouth and started chewing. I cupped my hand in the sink and drank some bathroom water. It tasted too processed, too chemical. I would have puked it up, but I had to get the pills in me. Thunderbird would have been better (figured then I would start to pack a bottle with me, just in case). It took a while in the bathroom, because I was trying to lose the suited ghost. I needed distance between us, and our relationship was getting to be too much.

After a good thirty minutes of faking a shit on the toilet, waiting for the Ritalin to kick in, I felt the comfort of the stimulant. I praised the winds by farting and crossing myself, by waving my hand and fingers over the four directions of my body, shoulder to shoulder, head, and dick (the sign of the four winds). I also saluted the sun by middle fingering the ceiling, and the moon by spitting on the floor. Now that religion was taken care of, I could leave.

I made my way to the bus stop and waited patiently next to a fat woman in green, and a ghost sitting next to her. She was retarded and her ghost looked after her. He saw my sigils and stayed away from me. I thought they were working well, so I made a show of them to the other passengers on the bus. They all seemed to like them, and kept capturing them on their handhelds and sharing the messages of power with each other. I was so wrapped up in spreading the sigils — my message—that I didn't notice my suited ghost was on the bus, near the back, where it always smells like pee and toothpaste.

I stopped and slumped back into my seat, tried to look forward and angle myself so that I could keep an eye on him through the driver's rearview. However, he's a ghost and he's good at what he does, which is haunting and sneaking. We pulled up to the Denny's and I casually got off. I looked back and he was following me. I came to the very real conclusion that I would have to talk to him soon. So, I waited until I got into a booth at Denny's. I had to talk to him, find out why he was haunting me. My luck, he picked a booth right behind me.

*   *   *

I didn't realize that Denny's was tantamount to purgatory, or possibly the real thing. I have yet to discern this fact as fiction or not. I was hungry and the pills were making my body shake as if I was having a fit, as if I wasn't right. I knew I was, but the waitress was a ghost and she was second guessing my order of coffee and pancakes. Maybe she didn't want to give me more stimulants. I needed them through the sugar and the caffeine. I needed them to stay sharp with the ghosts in there looking at me. Besides, I didn't have any Thunderbird. I kept my cool, though, even when my ghost—the suited one—sat down behind me. He ordered coffee from the ghost waitress, but she didn't acknowledge him. She just went to get the coffee he had asked for. Maybe the ghosts just didn't like humans ordering them around. Maybe the ghosts liked it when they had a place of their own, and from what I could see, this was their place.

The cook was a ghost, the other waitresses were ghosts, and I was getting too high off them all. I was relishing in the feeling, but it was also making me queasy. I needed food and Thunderbird and more Ritalin, but mostly food—for the time being—for I had taken three more Ritalin before I walked in the door. I also had to conserve, because I wasn't due for another batch until the next month.

When finally she brought the cup over, I took in a big gulp of coffee and it felt good. It helped with the shivering. It was so cold in there. Cold spots are a definite sign of ghosts (I read that in all the books on ghosts, which I took from the library). I waited to ask my ghost why he was following me until after I felt the shivering subside, but before I got my pancakes—a supposed never-ending supply for four dollars. At first he didn't respond, but kept drinking his coffee, looking out the window at all the other ghosts, scanning the inside of Denny's, and looking at all the ghosts sitting around. I needed to know why, so I kept on him.

Finally, he acknowledged me by telling me to "Shut the Fuck up, and mind my own fucking business."

I wasn't having this. Didn't he know I was alive? Didn't he know that he was dead, that he was to take orders from me? I kept pressing him, but he kept insulting me. He called me all sorts of names, and told me I was washed up. I told him I was high on Ritalin and his ghost essence. He threatened to punch me in the face. The ghost waitress came over and told me to quiet down, she told me to remain calm and that my pancakes were coming. She also said that I wouldn't get any if I didn't stop badgering my ghost, calling him "the other guests."

That was reasonable enough, but still, he was haunting me, he was following me. I told her to tell him, but he just laughed. My ghost was very condescending toward me. He insisted that he had never seen me before. I said he was a lying, filthy fucking ghost and that I would expel him from this world if he didn't stop. My pancakes came sometime in between all the things that we said to each other. Apparently, you can yell at ghosts in a ghost restaurant and still receive a delicious, never ending supply of pancakes.

I ate quickly. I didn't want to be vulnerable to a ghost attack. I shoveled the pancakes into my mouth and the ghosts looked at me in horror. I know they were thinking that they shouldn't serve me their delicious ghost food because I was human, but they can't discriminate, even ghosts follow the law of the land. My ghost didn't eat. I guess he wasn't feeling very hungry after I confronted him about following me, after he denied it. Guilt is a useless emotion—I learned that in Baghdad, too—but ghosts don't learn these things, ghosts don't fight wars, they send humans to do their dirty work.

He started talking to himself, while holding a black box. I'm almost one hundred percent sure it was a spirit box. You can build them and they scan radio frequencies, allowing ghosts to communicate with you through the white noise. I had one, too, but I never used it, didn't want to talk to ghosts, but had become privy to their secret conversations. I crushed up two more Ritalin on the table, and used a corner of the sticky placemat as a straw. After that, I heard the call to war.

My ghost was talking to the spirit box and telling it about me. It was calling more ghosts to come and get me. I would be easy enough to find, I was in purgatory, where they go to congregate, where they go to talk to each other. I looked out the window and realized that the more I looked, the more ghosts I saw. The more I scanned for real people, real humans, the less I saw them.

The ghosts were taking over. They all have spirit boxes, they use them to call their ghost brigades, then they seize the real people and they put them to work, or put them to death. I had already seen death.

I knew then that I had to act. I had to, they weren't taking me. I was going back to war, but at least I wasn't going to go to some desert or third rate country again, and if they wanted war then I would give them war, but it wasn't going to be on their terms.

I needed to liberate my human brothers and sisters. I needed Thunderbird. I had eaten and there was enough Ritalin in me to kill a horse, or some other such large mammal, though I couldn't be sure that there weren't ghost animals running around and capturing real animals, sending them to war, either. I never pondered that, I will later, and if I have to I will liberate the animals as well.

My ghost got up and laughed at me again, went to the counter and paid for his coffee, and then started pointing at me. I knew it wouldn't be long before the ghost brigade would be beating down the door, looking for me.

I needed to let them know that I knew, and that I was living, and that I wasn't going to take their schemes anymore.

I stood up and made my way to the counter, and my ghost moved towards the door. I pulled the pistol and grabbed him with my crab hand. I heard the ghost waitress scream, she must have been afraid in life. I pulled the barrel to his temple and wrenched his neck in the crook of my arm, like I had done before. However, it wasn't to ghosts, but to little women and children with bombs strapped to their midsections. They were probably ghost babies.

He strained against my grip up until he felt the barrel hit his temple. For being a ghost, he had a sizable amount of mass, but then again, we weren't in the real world anymore. We were in purgatory, and ghosts are tricky.

"Fuck this, I'm liberating my human brothers and sisters," I yelled.

The ghosts didn't know what to say, so they wailed and howled. They cried and pleaded, and I knew at that exact moment I had won.

"I'll banish you all. I'll exorcise the lot of you, starting with this one, if you don't tell me where you're keeping them," I yelled.

They didn't reply, they kept wailing, making noise. That's how ghosts fight you. They make noise and disrupt your soul. They keep you tied up in reality television, while they steal your insides and burn down your brain. I made sure my sigils were out to push them back, they stayed where they were. My ghost didn't move anymore. He began crying, telling me about his children, his wife, his home, his life.

I told him he was dreaming and that he stole those memories from the living. He kept crying, trying to convince me I was wrong. I almost believed him, but I held true. I told him I could set him free, could take him to the other side where he could go to the four winds, and then I farted out of respect. Religion must be kept up, along with order.

I was restoring order and belief, keeping the faith and holding the line, the line between real people and specters, humans and ghosts. I whispered in his ear that it wasn't his fault he was a ghost, kissed the side of his head and dug the barrel into his temple so hard that it pushed one of his eyes from its socket, and then I pulled the trigger.

The wail of ghosts at their fallen brother was enough to send me over the edge. I began firing into the crowd.

When I was done there were no more ghosts, there were empty shells, empty sausage casings. I let my ghost fall and I saluted the sun and moon, careful not to spit on my ghost. He didn't believe he wasn't worthy. Mother Nature knows I tried. After I was done, I overdosed on the ghost residue. I took their spirit boxes and their fiat ghost currency. I had liberated the Denny's. I had started the war.

*   *   *

I have met others, other people who get high off ghosts, others in the fight. We use our QR codes as both sigils against the ghosts, and to follow each other. We steal the old television waves and broadcast coordinates for our attacks, we hack ghost data farms and steal ghost identities. We fight them because we want them to know that we are real, they are ghosts.

Yet, I will always remember when I crossed over my first ghost. I will always remember the strength and sorrow of his eyes as he slipped to the ground.

The first time I got high off a ghost, I didn't really know I was getting high off a ghost, because I was drunk and running crushed Ritalin up my nose at three and four tabs a time.

My grave shall read this: I never wanted to be a freedom fighter, I just wanted to serve.

Salt Whispers and Blue Flowers
Nicky Peacock

I hate Summerline. She thinks she's too good to be my friend. She has Sidhe blood in her—a royal Fae—her magical powers were below that of other immortal Fae, but she holds her head like a woman who could defeat you with a curt nod. I'd been nice to her in the past, offered her assistance when she needed it, even cooked for her, made banquets for her parties and listened to her guests compliment her food. My taste was exquisite, intricate, demanding quality in my dishes.

I'd spent hundreds of years practicing my skills, did I get the credit? No. It was always "Summerline, what a wonderful salad, my dear. You have the best taste in the whole of the Dark Fae Court". I swear I could taste bitter ashes in my mouth every time I saw her. So, I stopped cooking for her, and so she stopped speaking to me, and we descended into social-civil fakery. When I was on my own, she never paid attention to me anymore, and there's power in that anonymity, freedom to pursue one's own thoughts.

It was on Court day that I saw them. I slipped in so close that I could hear all but every fifth word of her gossiping with her sycophantic, Brownie groupies. It lessened my hatred a little to hear their pathetic whispers, therapeutic white noise. I didn't want to appear as if I was listening, but I couldn't stop my reaction when I heard my own name. She knew. Summerline knew and she was telling those wretched Brownies.

Who else would they tell? Everyone. By sundown, the whole of the Dark Court would know, including our Queen (the Queen of Air & Darkness), who can suck the very air from your lungs. I always knew that they were trying to rid themselves of me, just didn't know how deep their hatred ran. They'd stopped inviting me to their dances and gatherings when I stopped cooking for them. I was only invited to the Dark Court because I was still one of the royal cooks and, of course, because I was a Dark Fae and legally had to attend.

You do one little thing wrong and suddenly everyone hates and distrusts you, like I meant to poison the Prince! It was at his very own bequest that I journeyed to the human world several times to collect new and intriguing tastes for his banquets. I called them my flavor adventures. I found many interesting things: fruits, nuts, vegetables, and fast food. Who knew those odious humans would use Fae poison as a seasoning? It doesn't just affect Fae you know, it affects humans, too. Yet, they sprinkle it onto their meals liberally, like white grains of death, each shake a step closer to the untimely demise of their short, pointless lives.

He ate one French fry and immediately convulsed, turned a bluish grey, and began to shrivel into a dusty puddle of royal Fae. It took the healers hours to regain his composure, thank the Deities that they were there, for if he'd been alone with the fry, well let's just say that the Dark Court would've been light one Prince! They never suspected the food. Being immortal gives you a certain sense of indestructibility that extinguishes your common sense. I worked it out, though, tested each ingredient until—through sweaty poisonous trials—I found the would-be Royal Fae assassin…salt.

Quite a shock for a lowly Fae Court cook to discover a weapon of mass destruction, especially as my Fae powers were less than impressive compared to Summerline. Yet, here I was with the perfect weapon and the perfect means of using it. I went back to the human world and, under minimal glamour, purchased cartons of that killer ingredient. I then used it to clean my sharpest, longest butcher knife. My gloved hands stroked the blade using the white, scratchy grains, and then soaked it in salty water until I was confident it could fell the most hardened Fae.

"Hello, I must say that this dessert you brought for the Court is the best I've ever tasted."

I was momentarily distracted by my friend, Raylune. Cream still laced his mouth and he spoke through a large quantity of mashed food. Food I had created.

"I'm glad you're enjoying it," I said, back bowing slightly. After all, I'm just a lowly cook.

"Well, I could have eaten one hundred more of them!"

What? Was he saying that I didn't bring enough? Had I underestimated the Dark Court's desire for fruit and sugar cream?

"I'll bring more next time."

"You'd better...they're delicious!" With that parting order, Raylune joined another group of gossiping Fae, no doubt to spread my culinary underestimations! Her laughter brought my attention back to Summerline. No doubt that the joke was at my expense. Both she and the Brownies knew everything about my salt weapon. I had to act accordingly.

After the Queen made her usual dribble-some speech, the Court began to disperse. I knew that Summerline would go back to her perfect little house, so I chose the Brownies first.

I followed three yards behind. They hummed melodious tunes and snickered to one another like rats talking over cheese. It sickened me to know that these lowly little scuttlers knew my secret and were laughing at it. I followed them deep into the dark woods, silently stalking, deviously planning, lost in a world of endless, dark possibilities.

They turned and looked right at me. I froze mid-step. They actually smiled, damn them. Even after they'd learned of my dangerous new power, and then bad-mouthed me to the whole Court, they were still patronizingly fearless.

"Hello," one said, moving toward me "We didn't know you lived this way. We'd have offered to walk with you."

"Yes," said the other, "journeys are so much better when taken with others, don't you think?" What new riddle was this? Were they mocking my loneliness, highlighting the fact that another Fae should be walking with me? Or worse – that I should lower myself to strolling arm-in-arm with gossiping Brownies?

Their practiced smiles dropped a little at my silence. I tried to smile back. It would all be much easier if they didn't know what was coming. I file my teeth pointy—they feel better that way—but sharp teeth make for an awkward smile, and I saw my sinister attempt at benevolence reflected back in their big brown eyes. I knelt as if to tie my shoe lace, but used the façade to slip out the knife that was sheathed along my shin.

They didn't run, funny that even toward the end they still thought of me as a harmless joke. I closed the distance between us quickly, grabbed one and threw her against a nearby tree. Enclosing my arm about the other,

I pulled her toward the knife. It made a satisfying sound as it slid into her gut. Sharp knives are such wonders. There was no resistance from either victim or flesh. Blood gurgled from her lips. She whispered something that sounded like "Why?", or maybe it was a parting insult.

As her legs gave way, I found myself toppling to the ground with her. That's when I heard the other scream. She turned to run, so I leapt up and began the chase. Brownies are quick little things, but have a tendency of leaning more toward hiding than running, shame for her really. If she had run, I would've never been able to catch up with her. Compared with *her* speed, it must've looked as though I was just strolling along in pursuit, my purposeful, murderous intent dancing behind my eyes.

She hid in a hollowed tree. I could see her heaving breaths coming from the bark. I pushed my knife in like she was a Brownie piñata. Brownies are not that hard to kill (after all they're not as powerful as Fae, and certainly not immortal), but their blood baptized my weapon, nonetheless. A slight tingle tip-toed up my spine, a weight that'd been squashing me lifted enough for me to breathe in the bloodied air of the woods. Suddenly, it looked all so very alive. Everywhere my eyes landed, I saw green life and warm fur, heard the hum and tick of the insects. It was the most alive I'd felt in over five hundred years.

I sat with the bodies a while. The sights and smells reminded me of when I was training to be a cook. My teacher—I forget her name—told me that to truly do justice to the meat, the chef themselves must kill the animals. The act of taking a life becomes the base of the recipe, and the need to make the deed worthwhile, inspires the cook to create their very best dishes. I made some amazing meals back then. It was no wonder that humans were told to never eat Fae food, for fear of nothing else ever tasting the same. Human food held more of an allure to the Fae, this deviation from the divine was what started the salty blood-soaked mess in the first place.

After a while, I buried the bodies. Brownies don't dust like Faes, so I couldn't allow the evidence to ruin me. Maybe I'd come back to their makeshift graves one day, and remember the battle of the Cook and the Brownies. I knew, then, that I was capable of killing more than just animals, and that the capability was born of a billion whispers I'd heard in Court, a billion fake smiles that hid contempt and pity. So, off I walked to Summerline's house, whistling as I went.

Her house was tall and frustratingly elegant. Yet, it had a door like any other, which opened without lock or announcing creak. I knew she was in her sitting room from the sickly smell of her sweet perfume wafting out. I must've smelled of death and blood, for she looked up to regard me with such surprise and horror. The knife reached, thirsty to taste Fae blood, as I moved quickly towards her. She ran.

She should've stood her ground, used her magics on me, but instead she tasted fear for the first time in her immortal life, and her instincts said run. She ran straight up her own stairs, not through the open front door. Where did she think she could go? An answer I'll never know, as I caught her mid-stair and slashed her pretty back, the knife catching on her sinew and bone. She looked fearful when she died, turning blue and dusting to a fine powder that lay across her elegant staircase.

Then, I went to her kitchen cupboard, retrieved her vacuum cleaner, and sucked her up. Couldn't let slip that a murder had taken place there, couldn't let out my secret. I emptied the bag over her colorful flower bed outside. All of the flowers vibrated and then turned a brilliant shade of blue. I never knew that could happen— no one did. How lucky for me that even without a body to visit, I can still come here and gaze upon those blue flowers, safe in the knowledge of my power.

I must admit that I felt a low after killing Summerline, especially as no one would know it was me who'd committed the act. I mean, what is the use of having power if nobody knows you possess it? Maybe I should pay a little visit to Raylune, bring him some more of that dessert he'd liked so much, find out what he's been whispering about behind my back. Perhaps, I'll open him up to see if he's filled with fruit, cream, and secrets. I bet he is—they all are you know.

Keep Your Feet
On the Ground
Jared Donald Blair

Mirna stood staring at the old picket fence where the
little white gate used to be. She outstretched her hand
and prodded forward with the tips of her fingers. A
smile broke her previously indifferent lips, as she pushed
aside the phantom gateway. Such a childish act seemed
appropriate, for the last sight of this property was
through the imaginative eyes of a nine year old.
However, her thirteen year absence meant nothing as she
strode, motivated by a teary-eyed joy. Almost
immediately, her mind began to swirl with vivid images.
She dropped her gaze to the dirt, yet dirt is not what she
saw. She envisioned the lush expanse of grass that once

existed beneath her feet, and saw the colorful crowding of plants and flowers that lined the yard. Her gaze danced upward.

Though the wood on the house stood decrepit and paint-stripped, Mirna looked on through a wonderful preadolescent veil. To her, the entire structure boasted an innocent white sheen outlined in pristine stripes of black and dark green: the way it used to be. The house—a three-storied Victorian masterpiece—used to catch the warming light of day perfectly. On those especially bright mornings the roof even seemed to glow. Mirna recalled her mother referring to it as a golden aura, but she always saw it as thousands of tiny luminescent wings trying to lift the house into the sky. To this, her mom felt it necessary to remind her over and over again to live in reality, uttering that usual phrase of hers—honey, please try to keep your feet on the ground.

An odd creaking resounded from the left, suddenly shattering her rose-colored lens. Ignoring it, Mirna again surveyed the house. Unfortunately, it did not shine as she remembered. It was now gray, just like the sky. Her eyelids constricted, breaking a welling teardrop and sending it prematurely down her cheek. Mirna watched its descent, as it was quickly absorbed by the earth.

Beside the slightly darker blot of soil lay a lazily coiled jump rope, its previous, almost neon-green hue now slightly discolored, tainted. She recognized the plastic heap immediately—not just as her favorite toy, but as the only one that truly embodied her childhood.

She bent to her knee, apprehensively. Though, the winsome smile on her lips hinted at how she felt inside: calm and intrigued. As her determined digits neared the rope's end, her flesh seemed to smoothen, every crack now filled, every scar now healed. Her fingers—once worn and hardened—met the plastic rope as tiny and delicate, almost dollish. Capturing the other end with her remaining hand, she straightened to a couth posture and lifted her wrists to either side. The grimy plastic, though obviously untouched for many years, dangled as lithely as twine to the tops of her shins.

Mirna stood with clamped eyelids, the rope's ends pressed to her fingertips only through the light pressure of her thumbs. Her hands bent back as far as anatomy would allow. The taut, paling, almost transparent skin on her wrists allowed the purplish veins beneath to reach daylight. She was once again a kid.

"A little too big for that, now, don't you think?"

Mirna's shoulders tightened. An ominous heat scored throughout her limbs, a series of tiny frozen pins in its wake. She dropped the rope and turned.

"Mother!" Her voice inflected with somber relief, the exclamation accented by the rope's furling slap against the dirt. Mirna ran up the porch steps and met her mother with a suffocating embrace.

"I've missed you," her mother let out, the tone sounding more of obligation than sincerity.

Mirna retracted, her arms elongated to her mother's shoulders, eyes moist. She re-administered the bear hug. "So many memories," she said.

Mirna breathed heavily. She bit her lips to keep them from trembling.

"Yes..." Her mother smiled back, caressing a rebellious strand of hair from Mirna's forehead back over the cusp of her ear. "But this isn't the same place, dear," she said, finally shying away from her daughter's impassioned hold.

"I used to sit out here for hours. I'd watch you play in the grass, the other kids on their bikes..." Her lips protruded, as if clamoring to put words to her waning memories, but instead her expression sank. "This place once had a life."

"Well…" Mirna tracked her mother's defeated gaze to the road. The cracked asphalt had long since relented to an uprising of grass and weeds, an unmistakable sign of Mother Nature's brute will. The houses on the other side were only vestiges of what used to be. The boards over the windows and doorways were prison bars, the *No Trespassing* signs were shackles. A notable gradient of degradation ran from left to right down the row.

Mirna's gaze returned. Her mother's eyes still sat unblinking within their sockets.

"Where's dad?" Mirna's words broke the silence, the question traveling laggardly into her mother's ears. Honestly, she knew and accepted the fact that her father was dead. She knew he had been for several years, but speaking of him as still alive always tended to cheer up her mom. It pained Mirna to humor her in that way—to only exacerbate the denial—but it kept her sane, and that's all that really mattered.

"He's inside." She gulped. Her features gained a new liveliness, but nothing substantial.

Mirna could hear the uneasiness in her mom's voice, could see the detachment behind her eyes, but again chose ignorance solely for her mother's sake.

"Let's go in," Mirna suggested, lunging one leg toward the front door. "I'd love to see what you've done with the place so far."

"Yes. I need you to help me with some of the work." Her mother's disposition softened with each word. "Your dear mother is getting old, you know."

A hint of playful sarcasm seeped from between her gaunt teeth. "But first, maybe a cup of tea?"

"That sounds perfect." Mirna patted her mother's upper back as she led the way into the house.

Once inside, her mother immediately turned left for the kitchen. Mirna, however, remained near the doorway. She swept the door to a close and stood reveling in the bare beauty of the interior. Her anxious attention ran over the walls and oaken molding, right to the sparsely furnished living room, straight ahead to the looming staircase, and left to the kitchen. Though stripped of all carpeting and warming adornment—essentially stripped of humanity—the entire place boasted a faint familiarity, the way a corpse resembles a living person. She thought of her dad and the way he looked in that casket, how she could imagine a smile over his stiffened lips. It certainly *looked* like the man who used to carry her on his shoulders. It *looked* like the man who'd once laughed so joyously at her silly stories. She tried so hard to pretend. It was the same way with the house.

Mirna's eyes never seemed to rest. She caught swift, phantomlike glances of her preadolescent self, sprinting from stairwell to sun room, swiping red crayon over the walls, placing her dolls atop the stair's banister to see how far they would slide before toppling over the edge. Truly, these were her childhood memories set in slow, residual movement, each one overlapping the previous. She looked to the debris filled buckets and poorly sealed cans of paint that lined the stairwell, as each heartening apparition began to fade.

These walls were far from convivial, but kingly compared to the devilish exterior.

"Mirna, dear." Her mother's voice crackled from the adjoining room, nudging Mirna back into the here and now. "I hope chamomile-lemon is all right, it's all I seem to have."

Mirna began toward the kitchen, through flighty feet and even flightier eyes. She wanted more time with the front room, but thought it rude to keep her noticeably stressed mother waiting.

"Yes, that sounds wonderful." She spoke while fingering back a sheet of plastic—the only separation between front room and kitchen—caring more about the cold, paint-spattered material than the flavor of tea. She smiled at her mother, procured a chair from the window-facing table, and sat. Mirna's mother laid a steaming mug before the both of them without a word.

"So, you think we can get this place ready for this weekend?"

Mirna pressed her palms to either side of the mug. It was far too hot to drink, but she didn't withdraw her hands.

"Ready enough." Her mom huffed, casting uneasy eyes to the ceiling.

She looked to the kitchen walls—the house's first outbreak of actual decoration—then to the old stove, the refrigerator, and the crooked shelving, anywhere but toward her daughter.

"This has been quite the burden, this...*house*."

Mirna knew her mother had wanted to say "this *damn* house".

"I don't know why I thought we could have it ready for the family reunion. Really, it was your father's idea."

Mirna's eyes crawled over the table.

"Where *is* dad?" Mirna surveyed the room from shoulder to shoulder, her efforts careless at best. It didn't matter, anyway, as her mother still wasn't looking at her.

"Taking one of his naps—you know your father. I believe he's up to three or four a day now." Her mother let out a long breath, mirroring the inconsistent hum of the refrigerator.

With her hands still cupped around the mug (they were just about numbed from the heat by then), Mirna dropped the subject and lifted her eyes. Through the window was the old pine tree, a twisted trunk housing many spiny branches. Strangely, it seemed as if the years had done nothing to the scraggly wooden monster—no growth, yet no deterioration.

"Amazing, isn't it?" Mirna's mom suddenly spoke, catching Mirna off guard.

"What is?"

"The tree. I was so surprised to see it still standing, after all these years. It seemed dead and rotted when we first moved in, but I never had the heart to take it out."

"Why's that?" Mirna couldn't remove her eyes from the crumpled bark.

"Why...?" her mother gave a supercilious chortle, "why if we chopped that thing down, you would have fallen with it."

The renewed liveliness in her mother warmed Mirna's disposition.

"We could never get you off that tree, I'm sure climbing it was your favorite thing to do."

"It was," Mirna said almost reflexively, her focus still fixed to the bare limbs. An ample, yet comfortable, silence followed.

"*You never fell...*" her mother's words came as barely a whisper, "it would never *let* you fall."

Mirna tried her best to peer out from the middle of the large window pane, avoiding the cloudy imperfections at the edges and corners. Again, she witnessed the apparition of her prepubescent self. The ghostlike Mirna forced her little arms to the lowest branch and, using the curled trunk as a foothold, lunged upward. She continued without faltering, not a single shaky leg or the curiosity to look down. The young Mirna had just about reached the highest bough, when again her mother spoke. The specter then melted gently, weightlessly, into the wind, like the fine ocean mist off a shore-bound wave.

"Well, perhaps we should try to get some work done around here." Her mother jostled her chair backwards.

"Yes." Mirna shook the fantasy from her head and followed suit. "Perhaps we should start with these windows."

Her mother's face took on a defeated scowl.

"I already did the windows," she said, her tone showing an uncharacteristic lightheartedness that Mirna always loved to hear, even a theatrically drawn frown to match.

Mirna looked to her mother with wide, embarrassed eyes, as a smirk began on the corner of her lips. It spread like the spark on a lit fuse.

After several silent seconds, mother and daughter joined in a duet of playful laughter.

*   *   *

Mirna stroked her paintbrush over the hallway wall in a calculated, but uneven, pattern. The sound was rough and aimless.

"What do you call this?" Her mother removed her brush from the wall, from a pristine covering of horizontal bars, and pointed accusingly to Mirna's masterpiece.

"It's..." Mirna stepped back, mocking an artistically inquisitive stance, "hmm...a seahorse. Yeah, look!" She giggled.

"Please just up-and-down, up-and-down." Mom mimicked her words with her brush, but as was usually the case, she couldn't help but succumb to her daughter's aloofness.

"So, mom, what is this year's theme? I can't believe I haven't asked you yet."

Every year the family reunion took on a different theme to dictate the attire, food, and decoration—a tradition developed to symbolize the togetherness in an otherwise distant family. Mirna always thought the idea was tacky—a means to keep conversation going rather than hearing the same old stories—but she always went along to keep her parents happy, which inevitably kept her happy.

"Ballroom dance." Her mother held onto the last syllable, not once looking up from her brushstrokes.

"Oh," Mirna said, surprised and genuinely pleased, "very nice."

"And I have the perfect dress for you already."

"Really?"

"Yes, it's upstairs on my bed, but—"

Mirna had already placed her brush into the aluminum container and met the bottom of the stair when her mother looked up.

"Oh, you're covered in paint." Her mother said more somberly than sternly. "Don't ruin it before you even put it on."

"Oh, mother."

Mirna climbed the stairway—occasionally skipping over two steps at a time—all but tripping her way to the apex, as downstairs her mother shook her head, but kept to her work.

Mirna found her mom's room. The door was completely ajar. She swaggered to the bed, on top of which lay an elegant, pale pink dress. Mirna pressed the sweaty tips of her fingers to the material and pushed down, enjoying the feel of the cool silk. She immediately lifted the dress by the ruffled fabric on the shoulder straps. Holding it out before her, a tingle scaled her spine. She loved it. She loved her mom. Her face was then captured by that recurrent teary-eyed smile.

"It's incredible!" Mirna yelled through the hall and down the stairwell. "Thank you so much!"

She heard her mother reply, but couldn't quite make out the words. Nevertheless, she held the dress with an unwavering gaze. At that moment, it was pure perfection in cloth and silk.

*   *   *

The two worked for the rest of the week on the house—cutting wood to replace the hollowed molding (the result of neglect and termites), painting over poorly spackled drywall, and scrubbing away at greenish mold and blackish stains—all the while reminiscing about the old days.

Mirna backed through the front door and onto the porch, carrying two plastic buckets filled to the brim with unusable wood, paint-smeared metal, and other assorted refuse. Her mother followed holding equally full containers. Mirna dumped the contents onto an ample pile of wood near the old pine tree. She stretched her elbows, peering up at the misfortunate house.

"It's a shame that we've worked so hard on the inside, when the outside looks so grotesque." Mirna spoke through heavy breath, her tone strung up by the usual sarcastic hooks.

"Well, there was simply no time," her mother replied, emptying her buckets as well as her lungs. "After all, it is what's on the inside that counts."

She shot an accomplished glare toward her daughter.

"Good one, mom."Mirna wrapped an affectionate arm around her mother's neck. Her body was exhausted, as was her mind.

"You hungry?" her mom asked.

"Certainly am."

"I think I'm gonna go start dinner." Her mother lunged toward the house, but looked back, as if awaiting a "*Need any help?*"

Mirna laughed at her mom's predictable antics. "I'll be in, in a minute."

She heard the front door urge to a close and stood in the magnificent solitude of the yard. The soft-spoken wind played with her long, curly hair. She shut her eyes and took several steps, relying only on her feet and her photo book memory. After venturing in—what seemed like—a yard-long half-circle, she stopped suddenly and opened her eyes to the dirt below. There lay the coiled jump rope.

She gritted her teeth behind a wide-eyed grin and bent down. Mirna slowly reshaped her spine and lifted the plastic rope, an end in each hand. She intended to continue from where she'd left off on her arrival. Her feet slid ahead of the drooping rope and her arms tensed, preparing for the first revolution. She felt graceful, elegant.

"Mirna, dear!" Her mother's voice rang urgently from the open kitchen window. "I could use your help about now, please!"

Mirna released the plastic with a subtle flick of her wrists and sighed.

"Coming, mom!"

*   *   *

It was finally the day of the family reunion, the fruition of Mirna and her mother's week of vigilant restoration. The cars began to arrive around one o'clock, each filled with members of the family that Mirna had not seen for many years, as well as several second and third cousins she'd never before met. She was delighted to see everyone, beaming wider at each oversized tuxedo and gaudy dress that passed. She actually saw it all as great fun.

Gentle strains of big-band swing spoke pleasingly through the newly installed stereo system. Mirna intermittently tugged at her dress throughout the night, more out of restrained nerves than discomfort. She mingled from one conversation to the next, laughingly undulating to the music as she went. Her grandfather chuckled after she told him that his tux looked quite snazzy—she did always enjoy the rhythmic bellow of his laughter.

She sauntered down the short hallway leading away from the living room. The slight scent of paint lingered in the air. A couple of her younger cousins stood staring and giggling at the large painting on the wall—a curious scene of a naked man posing amidst a gathering of dead trees—that her mom had picked up at a garage sale, earlier that day, for nine dollars. Mirna gave them a gracious smile and continued on, trailing her fingers across the wall as she strode.

Once through the hall, a tremulous sobbing broke faintly through the walls. Mirna realized that she hadn't seen her mother in hours, and deduced the voice, but not yet the source. She held her ear to every door before stopping at the laundry room. The door was open a crack. She edged it wider.

"Mom?" Mirna's throat quivered. The cries halted suddenly as the door swiped open, revealing her melancholic mother. "Oh, mom…"

"Hello, dear." Her mother cleared the blockage of snot from her nostrils. "Are you enjoying yourself?"

"Why are you crying?" Mirna asked, completely sidestepping the question.

"I, um…" her mother began, "I just can't believe your father isn't here. The whole family is finally in one place and he's missing it, sleeping." Another torrent of tears broke out.

Mirna embraced her mom and clung tightly.

"He's dead." The words slipped like vapor off her tongue. She had no intention of saying them, especially not then. In a fit, somewhere between empathy and embarrassment, she buried her face into her mother's shoulder.

"Mirna!" Her mom scolded, ripping away from the embrace.

"Don't say that about your father!"

There was an immediate shift from anger to sorrow. "He may have become a little distant in the last few years but—"

Her stream of consciousness forked. "I can't believe you would say something like that!"

Mirna turned abruptly to be sure her mother couldn't see the glistening tears on her eyelids. The powerless words "go to your room" came from behind her, but she knew it must have been mere instinct on her mother's part—the house, the anger, it was all a nauseating déjà vu. Staggering from the torrid laundry room, Mirna acquired and maintained a determined pace, hoping her mom would not follow. She knew exactly what she needed—a way to ease her head, as well as the sharp strain in her neck, and it certainly was nowhere in the house.

She yearned to finish playing with her jump rope, this time without interruption. Her ears perked to Sinatra's cool coos as she approached the front room, ignoring the salutations and pleasantries from the jubilant group as she passed through. She finally breached the stuffy cloud of perspiration and liquor fumes and reached the door. The act of pulling back the wooden portal and slamming it shut behind her felt strangely empowering. The silence was undeniable—she cherished it.

Where is it, she thought, scanning throughout the yard. Against patches of dirt, gravel, and weeds, surely an at-one-time neon green plastic rope would stand out. Mirna stepped down from the porch with wider eyes to the earth. She kicked at various sections of sod, as if the thing may be hidden under an invisible earthy tangle. It wasn't there.

It isn't anywhere, she thought, pumping her arms in frustration and tossing her head back. As the gilded strands of her hair wavered from vision, she froze. There it was—the toy of her current desires, coiled over the highest branch of the only tree in the yard.

"How..." She began the inquiry aloud, but finished it in her head.

The rope was finally in sight and nothing, not even the possibility of a thirty foot drop, would stop her. Mirna approached the old tree with a determined gait, as if the awaiting task was merely an everyday inconvenience. Stopping at its barky, rotund base, Mirna leveled her eyes up the trunk. Much to her surprise, it was just as tall as she remembered. Even the branches seemed to reach no farther than they did when she was younger. Lifting the skirt of her dress, Mirna placed a foot to the lowest bough and stretched herself up, wrapping her fingers eagerly around each woody protrusion as she went.

Nearing the median of her ascent, she stopped and rested on an especially corpulent branch where the main trunk split off in two. For some reason the house appeared less menacing from that height. She looked through the front windows. Everyone inside seemed so happy, either dancing or laughing, but she knew what would make her happy. Mirna continued upward, prodding at the hands and footholds, gingerly at first but gaining even more vivacity than before.

Almost there, she encouraged herself as the air around her began to whir. The jump rope flailed in the ever-increasing wind, seemingly berating Mirna from its higher perch. Yet, still she climbed, clinging tightly against the trunk to combat the weather. The thought of turning back was nowhere near evident in her mind. She scaled throughout the few remaining boughs, rather instinctively, until practically at the top. Though the wood creaked and whistled, she maintained her dogged composure.

The greenish rope hung precariously at the end of the highest segment, but for Mirna, fear had no power at that height. Without much hesitation, she straddled the branch and inched for the plastic rope. The wind tossed her hair over her head, but she gave it no attention—a few more thrusts and pulls, and she would finally be there. Her chilled fingers clasped the plastic and brought up the dangling end. She tossed it over her shoulder and made for the adhered end. The question of how it had come to be tied to the branch not once crossed her mind, but just when slack came to the knot, it seemed to pull even tighter against the bark. Mirna's frustration quickly turned to aggravation, then to sloppiness. The end over her shoulder repeatedly slipped to her bicep, forcing her to correct it. In one final fit of displeasure, she slammed the thing against her neck.

The plastic slithered across her opposing shoulder and over the front of her neck. It moved with growing rapidity until it accomplished several hard rotations. Mirna mindlessly brought her hands to the serpentine plastic. Though her throat incited a siren's yelp, the tightening vice cut off all breath, a perfect and sadistic retaliation. The rope's bluing victim shook but did not lose balance, that is, not until she was forced over the side. Mirna's face stretched and tensed, an expression normally accompanied by a rattling scream. Her body descended until the jump rope went straight. Though old and withered, the branch did not snap — of course, it would never let her fall. The vice held Mirna's cockeyed face to the sky, her favorite childhood plaything turned deadly ligature.

Her dress undulated in patterned waves as her legs thrashed, the disheartening motion accented by the squeak of her spine and croak of her throat. Her frantic eyes fell to the house. From inside, the noise of strangulation was less than a whisper. No one knew of Mirna's dire situation, no one even knew she had left the house. Her hazing vision then trailed to the near and intrusive moon, which she saw as a sinister skull, its jaw moving as if it was made of smoke. It mocked her as she convulsed.

Occasionally, a bubble of respiration would rise up from her mostly compressed windpipe, each time escaping her lips as a belched syllable: Mom.

These utterances rode piggybacked on currents of blood and bile. The sickening mess rolled down her chin and neck, plastering the pink of her dress in deep crimson. Eventually, it gathered at her ankles and dripped as shining red jewels to the soil below, a final guttural and bloody eruption. Her muscles lost all intensity and her beautiful, imaginative eyes turned inward.

Even in death Mirna managed to defy her mother, who time and time again told her to *keep your feet on the ground.*

Nazi, Retard, and Me
Abram S. Jacobs

"There is nothing new that anyone can write about!" my tall, husky Aryan-looking brother exclaims.

I swig my Molson, trying to contain the impassioned lightning within, pursing my thin, downturned lips so as not to explode at my well-meaning — but opinionated — youngster friend. "Of course there are new things to write about, otherwise, why are we here? What is the purpose? Words are like numbers on a giant combination lock of life. We combine the words in such a way that no one else has ever done, and the combinations are exponentially endless. What about passion? Of course new ideas and new things will be written to inspire us!"

A deadening silence follows. Crap, I did it again—mauled over my little brother who is bigger than me. When will I learn to shut up and give 'em some space?

Sniper's voice trails off as he recoils out the back door, holding his furry white dog on his strong left forearm. "Wuhl, our world is gonna end. We better get ready to live off the land 'cuz we're going back to the Stone Age." The door shuts behind him.

He was referring to his premonition and desire to see the fat cats in government and big business pulled from their high horses, to be like us common people who actually work with our hands for our daily bread. Sniper is a former carpenter who did a tour in Afghanistan, so he has integrity. I just misread his initial statement, thinking that if there are no new things to write, then it limits me from even writing this story. So, I write with a renewed passion, a sort of challenge for me to prove that yes — I can write something fresh, something unique, something true and strange. I hope that you will agree with me by the end of this story that what you experienced here is truly new.

Yet, remember that we may return to a base level of existence, whereby we depend again on one another, on God's natural surroundings as my humble brother Sniper suggests. I am sitting at the dark makeshift desk—glancing into the old Currier & Ives mirror—and realizing that this familiar unshaven face has not changed much in a half a century. If I haven't changed, then how the hell can I derive a new, interesting story? There are three rooms here on the top floor, joined centrally by a rustic kitchen of sorts. There are three separate tiny refrigerators—the Nazi strategically placed his close to his room and central to the kitchen, next to his shelf of food. The other two refrigerators are bi-racially stacked, with the black one on the bottom.

The sneaky Retard used to have his food in the black one, but slyly transferred his precious sustenance to where he could better reach it, on top, thus leaving me the dregs of the food chain below. Retard tried to snatch my room from me a day before I moved in, as his room is more of a hallway. He is a packrat with OCD—a weird combination. Retard only speaks with Nazi. I was officially renting the room for a day when I received a voice telegram from Retard via Nazi.

Nazi pleaded with me on the cell phone, "Please, please tell me you are going to go shopping for food today."

I smiled. "Why?"

"That Freakin' Fetal Alcohol Retard wants to know why there isn't any food in your refrigerator yet," he retorted. "I don't want to deal with this. I might do something to him that I regret, so please put something in your fridge today."

Initially, I felt like torturing the Retard by switching the positions of our refrigerators, or maybe placing his food into my cold space. However, Nazi advised against it by saying that Retard would not even understand. So, I resorted to taking Nazi shopping with me.

They say that first impressions are lasting impressions. My first encounter with Nazi was when I met him in a gay friendly town—strange since we are both heterosexuals. It was a rainy day and two feminine men were walking in the opposite direction from us across the street.

Nazi turned his head as if there was an auto accident to his left. "You fucking cocksucker fags! Keep walking, you are disgusting!"

I shook my head, but kind of laughed, too, as I never experienced anyone bold enough to speak like this. I later found out that Nazi was raised, in theory, as an East German soldier. I have known Nazi for about 20 years now, and his vulgarity has been tempered and his anger dissipated by time and medicine.

Retard, on the other hand, is a new type of acquaintance. On my first encounter, I did not meet him. Retard had his Idiot friend over on a Sunday night. His back was to me and he was mumbling to himself, while attempting to cook chicken.

"Eeeeyawoooyaaweee, I just burned my hand on the hot water. I stuck my hand in the hot water, eeeyaaawoo."

Nazi boomed, "Don't stick your hand in the pot. Use an oven mitt. You are using the wrong tool. Here, use this spatula to turn the chicken. And don't keep flipping the meat. Cook one side, then turn it and cook the other side."

Retard squealed, "Ooooh, wee, I uh…I, uh, burned my hand in the water. Oh, this one?"

The Idiot Friend of Retard glared at me and introduced himself.

"H…hhhi, my nnname is…"

Blah, blah, blah—I forget what he said. I just remember that he wore thick glasses and stammered. I escaped down the stairs before Retard even knew I existed.

I almost escaped notice on my second encounter with Retard, as well. However, Nazi made sure to introduce us. Retard held out his little hand and I went to shake it like a man, although not expecting any strength from this short, squealing, pitiful human. My hand touched his and his hand was unreactive. The statue of David contains more life than this Retard's hand or brain.

He doesn't even say anything. I usually match the opposing shaker's power, but his was less than zero, a negative amount, sucking the energy force from me. Yikes, I hope I didn't lose some of my IQ or DNA to this leech. Retard didn't stare, or glare, or see me. He wasn't preoccupied. It was as if he had so little voltage that the headlights of his eyes were burnt out. His brain is definitely not hooked up to his bodily system. He could be an alien in a human body. Yeah, that's it—he's a leprechaun with buck teeth. Not normal.

*   *   *

So, Retard's schedule is thus: up at six-thirty AM, carry radio into bathroom, sing while taking a long shower, "Lala...eee...waaaaa...(squeal)...dooo...daa...", straighten the silverware drawer—even though the utensils do not have a special plastic divider tray.

"Yeah, doo wee ya, spoon go on toppa' spoon, forkie on top of forkie, knife on the knife, yeah, good, good boy, did it, yooohoo."

Then, he checks to make sure the kitchen window is shut all the way and locked like Mommy told him. "Turn the twistie. Doo doo doo—got it."

Add some water to the dishwashing liquid. "Oopsie doopsie, someone um, forgot to uh, shut the cap last night, hee-hee. I click it shut again. Got it. Dee dee der mee."

Then, he gallops down the stairs to his S-10 super cab pick-up to work as an auto parts delivery driver.

Nazi tolerates the horrible mental troll singing in the shower, but has yelled at the Retard when the radio was too loud, or when Nazi is in a particularly bad mood. He usually awakens at seven-forty-five AM, just seconds after Retard leaves. Nazi checks the window to see if it was locked, sighs and swears, and immediately opens it wide for fresh air. It helps to ease his early onset emphysema, from exposure to Agent Orange in Vietnam. Next, he locks on to the dishwashing liquid.

"Damn it! That half-wit added more water to the mix. Arrgh! And the cap is down...idiot! I do all the dishes because I have my standards! I'm going to beat him on the back of the legs when I see him."

Nazi checks the floor between the shower and toilet. "That's it! That Retard pissed on the floor and didn't wipe it with the half-piece of paper towel like I taught him. I am going to beat that reprobate!"

Apparently, the last encounter concerning a wet mark on the floor was explained away by Retard. He claimed it was excess water from the shower, but Nazi said, "I know the difference between water and urine. Urine has a slight glaze when it lands on the tile."

Nazi intermittently naps and watches TV for a few hours, eating food in precision-cut increments. Sometimes he hangs out at the bus station, watching the dregs, hags, and beggars.

My schedule is: lay in bed listening to music, hoping my disability is approved, stay up extra late writing, playing guitar, and drinking coffee with my brothers. I slumber out of bed by eleven AM, make coffee, and sit at the green metal table with Nazi. I let him scream and tell me what physical harm he wants to inflict on Retard. I laugh at his rendition. I let him filter though his mad rants until he realizes that throwing Retard out of the window is not worth going to jail.

Instead, Nazi says, "I am supposed to love Retard like anyone else. This is a test from God. We could get someone worse if Retard leaves."

I nod in agreement, even though I laugh uncontrollably at Nazi's animations.

Usually, I take my laptop to a local coffee shop and plug in. I meet my brothers—Sniper and Genius—for coffee and conversation. I drive around a lot, unsure of what to do, sometimes meandering near the Orange River, checking out the tall pines and railroad tracks, sitting on the shale, watching the water swirl. Other times I sit at the mall looking for people to adopt me, hoping for someone—especially a pretty woman—to make eye contact with me. Maybe she would want to take care of me, if she only knew how depressed I get, lying for hours in my bed alone, with the music and sound of rubber wheels outside, constantly keeping me company. Those damn trucks are too loud…and the sirens! Nazi says that they purposely start the sirens exactly at our house, just to irritate him. He gives them the finger through the walls.

*   *   *

The third floor does have one mystery. There is a locked door at the top of the stairs, just before Nazi's room. I tried picking the lock once, as I'm naturally curious. Nazi once told me that it's off-limits to everyone, even him. He said the landlord keeps valuables there, and Nazi conjectured that it may contain six months' worth of supplies in case of a disaster. Still, it nagged at me for months.

Until, one afternoon when I was napping, I heard some light footsteps walking up the stairs. I knew it couldn't be Retard, as he was at work. I didn't think it was Nazi, as he shuts his door when he sleeps, and I didn't hear him that morning. The unknown person opened the secret door and I heard the shuffle of feet, as if the person was carrying something heavy. Then, I heard a muted thud. I tip toed quietly to my door and listened—whispering, like a Slavic language, a scraping sound like a trowel on a cement wall. I smelled sulfur!

I opened my eyes, but could not see. Was I blind? I felt my eyelashes sweeping across a familiar web material. Then, I felt an excruciating burning sensation, deep in my brain. What the hell kind of hangover is this? I tried to speak, but my dry lips would not move. I could only think.

"Eeehooo, I fooled everyone today, hee hee hoo hoo. I made believe I was gon'ta go ta' my job today and drive 'round and 'round again, tee hee um, but I did somethin' bad."

"After I fixed the house, I went downstairs, eyow…to the second floor, and heard some kinda' noise. I thought it was my um, doggie, my big doggie who died, wah. So, a door was open a little. Like Mommy said: if a door is cracked, I'm allowed to go in. 'Don't knock on closed doors!' Hee Hee. So, I slow-like open the big door. Wow, what a big door. Uh, like, I saw some man beating up the girl. They both were yelling. I had to stop the man from yelling. I yelled louder! EEEEEEEEEYYYYYYYYYYYYYYAAAAAA!"

"I jammed the pointy scissors on top of his head. That shut 'em up, heeya. The girl looked scared. That bad man hurt her. I told her that I would protect her now. She fell asleep. So I dragged the dead guy up to the closet. Boy, he was heavy! Then, I go back down and carry girl and put her in with my treasures. Hya. She is pretty without clothes. Okay, gotta' make love to her like Mommy

taught me. Don't let Daddy catch us...yikes! Girl wakes
up, I punch her asleep. All done, time to lock the closet.
Hee Hee. Late for work."

*   *   *

I wake up. What a dream! I was at a wedding. When I
lifted the veil of the bride, it turned out to be Oprah! This
must mean I need to be nice to black people today. God
gave me a 'no' on going downtown to catch the number
nine bus at ten-twenty, which connects with the number
twenty-one at eleven-thirty up to the mall. I watched the
Trinity Network preachers today. The end of the world
will happen on May 21, 2011, which is next Saturday. I
better eat my best hot dogs before then. I open my door
to the common area and find a speck of blood on the stair
near my room.

What the hell? That Retard probably cut himself
shaving and went to work all bloody, the stupid half-wit.
Better put on my rubber gloves before cleaning this mess.
I check the window, dishwashing liquid, and bathroom
floor. Shit, there is a lot of blood on the bathroom floor,
like the Retard cut his wrists. That would be too good to

be true—ooops, sorry God! You don't like that. You're right—forgive me—but that Retard pisses me off. Why would we need to populate the earth with more of him, though? He drains the economy and the quality of life.

I go downstairs to check the mail—nothing yet. I hear groaning from the hall near the front door. My landlord Jack is lying face down with a pair of scissors in his head. I don't want to be blamed, so I run upstairs, grab my Italian made .45 caliber, and do the mercy thing. Hope the Brotha's outside don't react to the shot. Jack dies immediately. I decide to put the body in the Retard's room—such a likely perpetrator. No house can be clean enough.

I come home from my half-day of work, hee dee doo dah. I bound up the stairs—um—did I really use that word, "bound"? Hey, the Nazi is teaching me new words, yay. I fix the window, lock it. I fix the dishwashing liquid, snap the top. I pee on the floor—*wheee!*—just enough for Nazi to clean. He's my new Mommy. Screenew, mowie. I check my room—um, yew, hey…who put J…jack on my bed, and how did my scissors get t'in his dumb head? Oh well, nee naw no more rent to pay. Free! Hee-hee-hoo, just me and Nazi, and that other guy…um, name I don't know…okay, la-laloo. I will call him Dead Guy because I'm gon'ta kill 'em up today. Wee la, I wanna just me and Nazi live here, huyuck.

I take the scissors from Jack's brain. OOOOOweee, oldie brain smell like tuna and burned coffee, ho. New Guy's room — creepy in, hee-hee-ha. He is napping. I go close to him. Uh-oh, his eyes open. I plunge pointies into tummy, doo-ya. Then into eyes—Beeya! Jam Jam. He's cryin'. Big Baby. Ouch, stop his squeezing my wrists— *oooo*—that hurts.

Crash! I am flying through the air, head first like Superman! Hee-hee! Um, oops, sidewalk....

*   *   *

The soft spoken nurse says, "It's time to remove the bandages, Honey. You will feel a little discomfort."

Suddenly, the darkness lifts from my left eye, the sound of medical tape being torn from my face. *Yeow!* God have mercy! The pounding in my head continues.

With one eye I see an angel smiling. "Hi, Sweetie. You gave us a scare."

A male behind her speaks, "Yup, he was living in the abandoned house by himself. Cops found forty-two bodies in the locked room. He may have been next."

I discover that I blacked out for a while! The nurse was actually my wife who'd been looking for me—a missing person for three years.

My wife asks me, "How are you feeling, Honey?"

I quietly answer, "Eeeeeeya woo doo, hee-hee. Um, I, me is okay. I been with my Mommy, right? I have always been with you...you fuckin' Retard."

When it comes down to it, there is a ceiling to our intelligence. In reaching the top, somehow it seems to shatter—and we become like cavemen, throwing stones at glass houses.

The Ostrich Nest
Todor Oluic

I am a saint.

I have reached a level of bodily inhibition of which some only dream. If my body is a temple, then mine is open to all.

I am a saint.

I have cured ailments. Deprivation subjugated to the laws of abundance by breath I bestow on those denied portions.

I give of myself altruistically and without chains. I make no puppets of my conquests and make no trophies of those who hunt me. My skid marks are left on the roads I trod before. Highways paved with crystal gold. They are all gold.

I know what I have done and what I fail to do, although I know I will be absolved in days to come.

I have studied faith. I have studied science. I have studied history—a clear mixture of the two previously stated fields. I believe that science is mixed with faith to make history.

I am a saint.

I derive the title from a book I read. No, I didn't. I'm also a chronic liar. No, I'm not—maybe just a hypochondriac.

What's *my* name? Well what's *your* name? Terry? Max? Jake? Something that rhymes with Doug, no doubt.

The following events are completely true for me. Factual. Honest. Real. Redundant. Even as I write these thoughts I see a tear duct on the horizon, ready to release its burden. Not out of sadness, but out of ecstasy. Ex. E. Most of that shit is filler, anyway.

Drainer fluid. Anti-Freeze. Bird beaks ground of dust. Cough medicine. Orphan tears. Prison guard sweat after a beating. Hot sauce. Alcohol. Pen ink. Grief. Pages of *Beautiful Losers* by Leonard Cohen. Sea water. Marshmallow marrow. Manna from heaven. Gold. Shoelace smell. A smiling poet's shaved pubic hair. Opera singer spit. Field trip forms. Cocaine. Sandpaper gun triggers. Ripped up condom bits.

I wasn't always like this, though. When I met Veronica I was a kaleidoscope. A rhapsody of ghosts. Drastic weather. A meteor storm in the eye of a suburban cream. An inhibited mood swinger. A cosmic blob of musical belligerence. A quantum creature of multidimensional fornication, peeling, wheeling, stealing color and form from the hands of a derelict space vessel, taking its fuel to oil myself up.

Veronica would hold on tight and twist me around, all the while enjoying her mirror and glitter peep show, scouting out her next Egg to solidify by her tests. Oh, a painless student was I. Number two pencil, three ring binder, ten and a half by eight inch paper. Studious and diligent, with the perseverance of a university student, but the shyness and tender skin of a high school freshman. An easy target. Repressed ejaculation. Hairless hands. Street signs on my loins. Leafy lips of lily pad. I was a challenge, and she was the Reaper. A whole book lies in her house and all her conquests imprint the pages, but the book never ends. It had no back cover, no final page. I was just an addition. Not a beginning or an ending, just a continuation of the epic tale she read to herself at night to help her sleep.

"Be uninhibited," she says. "Fuck all, love none," she chimes. "Be a teenage cupid, whose arrow can't distinguish between sex and love," she spits.

Am I done yet? Have I reached that level of freedom? Is the whole world white? Some kaleidoscope. I'm focused now. Focus pocus. You need focus. We need to find the Egg. Veronica found the Eggs time after time, after time, after time, after time, after time. After a time I got scared that I wasn't me anymore, but I'm always me. No one stays the same forever, but it's always you.

Fickle Friend. KKKing. Silver Servant. Beautiful Beatnik. Jinxed Jock. Paroled Paramedic. Hawaiian Haberdasher. Dreamy Druggie. Reckless Robot. Apple Antagonist. Crude Creep. Quirky Quitter. Xenophobic Xylophonist. Plastic Preacher. Salty Singer. Lustful Laundromat. Braided Beard. Vindicated Vaudevillian. Gamely Greeter. Omniscient Orthodontist. Free Firefighter. Tibetan Taxidermist.

Sometimes I forget, but she drives it home.

Before I met Veronica I was a simple psychiatrist. I would assess the gray areas—their diameter, their centers, their maximums and minimum—and I would log them into my brain. Then, my patients would come with their flamboyant auras and it would be up to me to repaint the masterpieces they call their minds, and dilute the pastel regions to more monotone flavors. It was just my job. Then, I found Veronica.

She came into my office one day—yellow teeth mapping out her world—claiming to suffer from hypochondria. She was a five-foot-seven monster on wheels, but of course I didn't notice until much later (or you could make the argument that it was more willful blindness than sheer ignorance). I asked her what her favorite activities were and she said, and I quote, "Sandpaper gun triggers." I asked her what sandpaper gun triggers were and she answered, and I quote, "Shit you like that don't do you no good."

"So, you're a masochist?" I asked.

"Naw, I'm a hypochondriac. Didn't you hear me the first time? Shit, for a shrink you need to improve them listenin' skills."

Within a year we were married, but instead of wedding bands we had halos, and instead of a dress and tux we wore black eyes and dirty feathers. We weren't in love, we didn't have sex, but there was some bond there—something that put us in the same bucket of chum, some notion we found in one another to which we could relate.

When I first saw Veronica's dust breeding neighborhood and apartment I should have been appalled. It was the grimy underbelly of a suburban engine, where all the drug hungry ostriches lived. I was so entranced by the cocaine sprinkled rawness of the lifestyle that a week later I emptied my bank accounts and burned my house with all my belongings, save for seven outfits (one for each day of the week).

It was the first step in my advancement into sainthood.

*   *   *

Now that the nest was home to two flightless birds instead of one, I needed to carry my weight. So I decided to "fuck all, love none", as Veronica had once told me during one of our sessions, and begin selling my body. My savings wouldn't last forever.

Through sexual inhibition I was able to not only to get some green, but also some red. I was surprised at the market for males of the oldest profession, and after a while I even opened my borders to ships of all varieties. In a way, I was again a psychiatrist. When someone wanted a prescription, I'd give them a pill—men, women, gays, straights, and everything in between. All of my patients had their own ticks and triggers they expected me to pull, and I never disappointed.

"We don't do this for them," Veronica said. "We do it for us."

I asked her what she meant.

"Mankind's a joke and it's starting to recognize. That's why people like the shit we do to 'em, they dunno' what'a do."

Veronica, though not a hypochondriac, was a born and bred, through and through nihilist. That's why she did the things she did—the drugs, and the sex, and the monster peddling. She saw herself as a non-existing void of static, and that it didn't matter what she did to her body because it wasn't real. When she was still my patient, I asked her what I ask all my nihilistic patients.

"Why do you think bad things happen to good people?"

"Think of it this way," she replied. "When someone got lice it's usually 'cause they clean, not 'cause they dirty. Lice love clean bitches. E'reyone's always like: 'bitch dirty 'cause she got lice', when really the du'e with the lice is probably cleaner than the du'e without." She picked her teeth with a dirty fingernail when she was done talking.

It was the most interesting answer I'd ever heard, and a contributing factor to my sainthood. She convinced me. She convinced me that God had fucked up. It led me to realize that I indeed was a joke. So began my self-abandonment.

*   *   *

I did drugs, not to feel good, but to feel nothing. Feeling was a mistress without censors and I wanted to cancel her, reinvent my channel. SSDDTV-23.5 didn't need her riffraff to bring in the ratings. My viewers didn't need to see Feeling. So, Veronica and I would sit there—apathetic and breathing in the formless car exhaust—avoiding Feeling at all costs. Until one night, Feeling slipped between the barricades and began to spread.

I couldn't take it. I had to get out. I left my four walls of gray solitude and entered the meditative night. I walked to clear my mind, but Feeling would not submit so easily—this bitch was a fighter. So I let her run. I came upon a little cafe and entered. I came to the front desk, where a cashier stood as if she'd never heard of Egypt, Japan, Libya, or Haiti.

"May I take your order, sir?" She asked, the smile grating my eyes.

"Just a water," I said coldly. water was free.

"Right away, sir."

She got me my water with a nylon grin, and I walked away without a thank you. I sat at one of the tables and began to drink my water from the white mug. A song was playing on the radio, but the only words I could make out were some Bible-thumping-ranting. This scene was too perfect: A silver-screen landscape of a man sitting in a cafe, taking his drink too seriously while listening to Christian rock, reassuring him that all things happen for a reason. It was too perfect. I got sick of it, finished my water and left, throwing myself once again into the cold, comforting street lights.

My ascension left me floating through the world like a ghostly castaway in a reckless sea. Despite my self-abandonment every feeling I'd ever experienced, or tried to repress, flooded back and began to lay their Eggs under my skin. Larvae were hatching, and crawling, and feeding off of my high—replacing it with emotion. My insides were squirming. I heard God in every passing car, in every buzzing street light, in every fallen footstep. All my senses were choppy like some experimental techno song in which I couldn't find the rhythm. Not until I found the Homeless Man did I focus and at long last reach the final phase of my sainthood.

He was next to an alley holding a cardboard slab, his sad eyes and gloved palms revealing more than any biography ever could. What was written on the cardboard angered me. So out of spite for him, I walked to the alley and grabbed my own piece of cardboard, and a dirty piece of a broken mirror. I used the shard to cut my finger, used my blood to write my response to this man's silliness.

His sign said, "*Repent*".

Mine said, "*HAHA*".

We stood facing each other, without speaking, my eyes angry and his eyes sad. After an hour of standing my legs became weak—they weren't what they used to be. Why repent? Who's listening? Who's going to absolve us, some fucking ghost-dad? Too late, he fucked up. Then, I had a thought. It inserted itself within me, rummaged in my mind and tore out all my fears and anger and insecurities, laid them all down in the sun to dry out.

The thought was: Who cares? Is it I that exists, or all that I wish I were? Did it even matter? I was a saint after all! I was so free of blockades that I had abandoned my body until I was just an echo. Now it was time. I was ready to get some questions answered. God couldn't hide behind the stars anymore, because I was coming up there. I threw my sign in the gutter, where it dissolved like my body. I gave the Homeless Man the middle finger and stepped into the street. I opened my arms to give the oncoming bus a great big hug.

I closed my eyes and felt my body disperse like a snowflake in the ocean. One calm echo of a thought drifted between the droplets of sadness and anger and confusion, a thought that I knew to be true because of what I'd accomplished in my time with Veronica, living in the home of flightless birds. This thought was all I had when finally I dissolved.

I am a saint.

First Assisted Suicide

Leonora Stein

A knife doesn't have to be stylish, you know, just sharp. I took the knife from my neighbor's kitchen, a simple carving knife meant for meat. After that, I only had to look for a suitable sharpening stone. It only has to be large and smooth. I found the perfect one at Coney Island and cut my fingers up plenty of times sharpening that knife. It was so sharp that it could draw blood without causing pain. So sharp that it whistled when—while practicing how to handle it—I swung it down. It was my prized possession, and I hid it under my bed to keep it safe until the time came.

He came to me in early September claiming he had some sort of cancer. This may have been true, for he was basically bald, and very thin. He'd threatened to expose his therapist as a child molester, unless the shrink told his parents that he still went there every Tuesday, Thursday, and Saturday, instead of to my house. He was young, which surprised me because he had a voice too low for fourteen. He was a kid, and became offended when I laughed at him. How could this scrawny, pubescent wimp have the guts to kill himself? Well, that was the problem really. He didn't have the guts to do it.

He wanted me to do it for him, and he had no preference for how it should be done. I always thought that if you're going to die by your own will, you've probably fantasized about it quite a bit. Yet, he was so shaken by the whole idea that he told me to choose.

"It'd be easier on me if you just gave me a gun or something," I told him, but he didn't have one, not a middle class wimp like him. What luck?

"What can I tell you, kid? You don't sound very serious to me."

He assured me that he was extremely serious, that he'd thought about it long and hard and just didn't know how to do it. I suggested hanging, pushing him off a cliff, drowning, but he refused by saying those sounded painful. He wanted to die painlessly—spoiled brat.

"Why don't you just take some morphine and come back to me?"

That's when he suggested the knife. I warned him it would be painful—especially if either one of us fucked up—but he was adamant. That was the way he wanted to go.

"Where am I going to get a fucking butcher's knife?" I asked him.

*   *   *

So, we devised a simple breaking-and-entering plan that enabled us to steal a large carver and some jewelry from my next door neighbor, the chef. The jewelry was the kid's idea. His parents were deep in debt from all the hospital bills and he wanted to help them out. I had no problem with this since it would derail the cops, and because the woman we were stealing from had enough jewels to satisfy a Park Avenue army.

Her name was Mrs. Barker. She kept the name from the guy she had divorced five years before. He begged to be able to see their daughter, and she only agreed because of that alimony check. Then, three years after the arrangement, Mr. Barker ups and has a heart attack, leaving Mrs. Barker with the house, the country cabin, and gobs of money.

Recently, she went around the neighborhood tacking up signs, advertising that she was in need of a babysitter. I, realizing the opportunity, ripped one of the slips off and called my diseased friend. The next day he called Mrs. Barker and told her he was very good with children. She fell into our plan perfectly, asking him to come over two days later. She told him to put the little princess to bed at nine, and that she would be home around two or so. Often, I noticed that she didn't come home until three or four. Mrs. Barker likes her fun.

I waited until midnight to cross over the roof to her brownstone, wearing only black and brown. My friend had graciously unlocked the roof door and I found it easy to climb down the metal stairs and through the attic to the fourth floor. He was waiting for me to descend from the ceiling there, his wide eyes shining blue, body shaking with excitement. I told him to shut up and calm down, and carefully walked down the creaky stairs to the kitchen on the first floor. There, I found the one I wanted and was just running my finger over the edge, when the kid practically jumped me from behind.

"Hey! This is so great! I've got such a rush!"

I shrugged him off. The blade was too dull, but I took it anyway, already thinking of combing the beach at Coney Island for the perfect whetstone. He followed me all the way back up the stairs.

"Can we do it now? I'm fucking serious. Let's just do it! Right here!"

He was so excited, he was sweating, hanging onto my arm like he was about to fall into a never-ending pit. He was terrified he might slip, yet longed for it. His eyes were brighter than ever and filling with tears.

"Stop it!" I whispered. "We're not going to do it here." My voice was derisive—I could see him deflating already. "Anyway, it's much too dull. It would hurt."

He backed away slowly, breathing deeply. I noticed he was trying to suppress a smile. It occurred to me for the first time that the cancer could have reached his brain.

"Okay. I don't want it to hurt. But promise me it'll be soon—real soon."

Two months and twelve babysitting gigs later (I convinced him to steal the jewelry one piece at a time) and we were ready. Both of us had been busy. I spent most of my days in my room, mesmerized by the movement of the blade as I swept it up and down the stone—one side, then the other, one side, then the other. It possessed hypnotic beauty, and after a few screwups—which involved some peroxide and bandages—I'd gotten the rhythm down like a machine. At night I would sharpen to the tune of the television, and sometimes in the morning I'd eat breakfast one-handed. I was in love with it.

The kid was busier, I'm sure. When you know you're going to die at a certain time on a certain day, you become more frightened than ever. Sometimes you see yourself at a distance, remarking in your head how cool, how fucking cool this is. You know what's going on. You're controlling your own death. Yet, there are other times you may be walking down the street, or lying in bed, when you realize the full weight of the decision. It's no longer cool and dangerous, because you realize you've never seen the world through anyone else's eyes, and soon those eyes will disappear. You begin to doubt the reality of the world around you, begin to feel that the moment you go, the world goes, but that's not true. It will exist without you and you will be what you once were: nothing.

He was more level-headed than I would have been in his shoes. Firstly, he wrote a will. I know this not only because he showed it to me, but because I was in it. However, I put an end to that.

"Are you fucking nuts?" I exploded. "You can't write my name down. Don't you think your parents will be a little suspicious of someone they never heard of? Especially, if you're leaving them a knife!"

So my name was stricken from the will, but he told me in person I could keep the knife. I told him right back that I was throwing the fucking knife down the sewer system, did he think I *wanted* to go to jail? Maybe he was having a little trouble remembering that we were all going on without him. I didn't want to be cruel, but I didn't see the point in painting any romantic illusions of what we were doing. He was hiring me to kill him— plain and simple. That's why I didn't see why he wanted to leave a note. In the will he claimed to have killed himself, but he was a kid, so what do you want? We're all romantic at that age. That was the only time I saw him mad.

"It's my death and I'm leaving a note. The will is business. The note is personal."

I said okay. I wasn't going to tear it up when he was gone, and he assured me that he'd repeat it was a suicide in the note. He was sure his parents would buy it.

"Let's do it tomorrow. I'm ready."

By this time the skinny fourteen-year-old—who'd knocked on my door two months before—was a fifteen-year-old with a few strands of hair left on his head, and a body twisted in pain. He needed to take twenty different pills a day, and his parents were making arrangements for his final stay in the hospital. The doctors, he'd overheard, were giving him about a month.

"I'm fucking serious. I can't wait anymore." He could hardly walk and I wasn't sure how we were going to get him to the designated spot. We hadn't planned on him getting this close to death.

This was the one hitch in the plan. The jewelry was hidden in his closet, in a box that read: OPEN. FOR MOM AND DAD TO PAY BILLS. Mrs. Barker had been told he was away at summer camp for eight weeks. The knife she never missed, but the jewelry she reported stolen and a reward was offered, something like five thousand dollars. However, the burglar left no prints belonging to a known criminal, and the case was soon dropped. The insurance paid off the items and Mrs. Barker was content to forget it.

Everything worked out except for one thing. My little shrimp of a friend was sick, really sick—coughing up blood, and fainting sick. If he wanted to kill himself, we knew it had to be soon.

"What are you waiting for?"

A warm night in November, I carried him fifteen blocks to the alley we'd decided on. It was an industrial area, uninhabited at three in the morning. There was a train station only a few blocks away, so it was the perfect setting. It was dead quiet. I lowered him to the ground, where he gained his balance by holding onto a wall. He looked steady, almost strong. I took one more look around, but there was no one in the whole neighborhood. Far off, I heard a boat on the East River.

He smiled at the sound. "You got it, right?"

I nodded and drew the blade from my coat. It was so sharp that I wrapped it in a dish cloth to save myself from being cut. It actually glinted in the light of a street lamp. I felt like I was in a movie and suddenly had no idea what to do next. He seemed less worried.

"You're going to do it, right? You're not scared?"

"No," I said, "I'm not scared. I'm worried."

"Let's just do it—now."

I advanced on him and he instinctively moved back a step. We were both deadly serious. No one was smiling. He gripped the wall tightly, so that he wouldn't fall. I knew he wanted to be standing up at the time. I was so near to him that I could feel his ragged breath on my neck. My God, he was so much smaller than me, probably weighed seventy pounds. His face was white and drawn, and his hand was gripping my arm so that he wouldn't fall. He seemed to be begging me for something. I had the knife in my right hand and as I raised it, I accidentally hit his chin and cut him.

"Sorry."

"No, it's okay," he said.

I pressed the tip of the knife against his Adam's apple. It was the easiest way to go—cut the jugular and he'd be unconscious in ten seconds, dead in forty—but a sound startled me, and forced me to turn. The tip flashed on his throat and his breathing grew faster. My left hand on his neck, him still clinging on that arm, was holding his blood. The sound was nothing, wind whipping through a plastic bag. He was terrified. It was taking longer than both of us expected.

"Please...I swear I'm ready. It hurts like this. Please, please."

I faced him and took my hand off his neck. The blood came out so fast that drops flew at my arms, face, and hair. There was something wrong with his voice. He sounded as if he was choking.

"Go, go. I'll close my eyes."

When he closed his eyes that made it easier, and I quickly sliced the knife through his throat. His grip gradually relaxed on my arm, the other hand released the wall. I let him down on the ground. He was still alive, but barely breathing. I never knew that the human body could hold so much blood. It was everywhere. It covered the small alley and my clothes, my face, and my hair. Luckily, I was prepared. Looking around quickly like a crazy person, I took out the sealed envelope that held the reasons, I suspected, for this situation. I knew he was carrying identification, so the note must have held other information, personal information. Suddenly, I wanted to know why—besides cancer—this young man had decided to ask someone to kill him.

I didn't open it, but dropped it by the kid, far enough away so that it didn't fall in a pool of blood. It got spots on it, anyway. I knelt down to say goodbye, careful not to make bloody footprints. I couldn't say anything, though. So I backed away, got businesslike. I carefully took my outer clothes off and put them in a plastic bag. I covered my hair with a hat and changed my shoes, pulled off my bloody leather gloves and placed them—along with everything else—inside my book bag. Lastly, I wiped my face and arms with a damp washcloth, and checked my hands. They were clean. The kid was unconscious and probably dead.

I suddenly felt conspicuous, spotless next to all that blood. I looked around and then took off from that alley, walking not running. I had a token with me, so I didn't have to deal with the clerk in the booth. The train was basically empty. There was one man, but he didn't look at me and I didn't look at him. At close to five in the morning (just about the time the fishermen are waking up), I arrived home. In another couple of hours he would be found.

I threw my bloodied clothes out and washed the knife until it was clean, and did not look like it had just killed a boy. The next night—after sleeping for fourteen hours—I duct taped the knife into a sewer. The grate was broken and, when no one was looking, I found a place on the ceiling where it couldn't be seen from the outside. By the time the water loosens the tape, years will have passed, his funeral will be long over, and an old, rusty knife will be found by the sanitation department.

Topeka
Scott Barbour

I cut to let the evil out.

The scars crisscross my forearms like tic-tac-toe games, one on top of another (the older ones thin, white, and pink; the newer ones thick, red, and purple). One day at lunch I show them to my friends. We're in our usual spot—P.F. and Duane and I lined up on the ground, with our backs against the wall of the auditorium, Jocelyn walking back and forth in front of us. I raise the sleeve of my sweatshirt to expose my slashed-up left arm to the October sunshine.

"Whoa!" P.F. says.

"*Damn*," says Duane.

Jocelyn stops pacing and looks down at my arm. She lifts her sunglasses to get a better look. Our eyes meet for a moment, and it feels like she's finally seen me. "Motherfucker," she says.

The following Friday night I take Jocelyn to a stupid second-run movie. Afterwards, I drive her around in my old green Nova. We cross the river to East St. Louis and park on a dark street near the lake. This is what I've been wanting for the past year. Jocelyn's lips are thick and plump, like the petals of some exotic jungle flower, and kissing them is even better than I imagined. The windows steam up from the heat of our bodies. She grabs me and everything's fine, but then I stop. It's like a switch gets thrown inside me and I go empty. I turn away, wipe the side window with my hand, and look out at the halos around the streetlamps.

"What?" she asks.

"Nothing. I just..."

"Just what?"

I shrug and lean my forehead onto the cool window glass.

"Whatever, motherfucker."

I drive her home in silence. When we get to her house I say, "Sorry. I don't know what my problem is."

I grip the steering wheel, the engine running, as she stares at me for a long time.

"Yes, you do," she says.

She's right.

What's wrong with me is Carl (my mom's ex-boyfriend), who fled in his red Grand Am a year ago, but still haunts my life. My therapist, Karen, says it's like I was in a cult. She explains it all to me—how Carl messed with my head, took over my thoughts and turned them against me. She tells me it wasn't my fault, I was a victim and there's nothing wrong with me. It makes sense when I'm in her office, but in the outside world nothing makes sense. My heart feels like rotten meat. I'm broken and I'm sure everyone sees it, even though I only told my mom. I hear kids laughing at school and I know it's at me.

I wake up thrashing and kicking, drenched in sweat. I try to stay awake to avoid the dreams, but they track me down. Sometimes it happens while I'm awake, walking to third period physics or sitting in the TV room. I hear Carl's voice or feel his hands on me. It's happening again. I freeze up, lock down—lose large chunks of time.

Cutting brings me back and snaps things into place, restarts the clock.

My mom checks my arms every day. When she sees fresh cuts, she tugs me into the bathroom and cleans them with an angry kind of love. She cries but doesn't say a word, doesn't ask why.

Jacob, my little brother, begs me to stop. "Why can't you just be normal?" he asks. I'm glad he doesn't understand—that means it never happened to him.

On the day Jacob turned 12, the age I was when it started, I told my mom what Carl really was. Carl left as soon as my mom started yelling. She says he's long gone, but I'm not convinced. Some nights I can feel him out there, thinking about me, feel him coming back.

One night I wake up and I know he's in the house. I jump out of bed and turn on the light. I check my closet, under my bed. I search the whole house—the kitchen, the pantry, my mom's room, even the attic, shining my flashlight into the corners. The place I'm most afraid to check I save for last. I slowly open the door to Jacob's room, silently step inside and shine my light on him. He's sleeping on his side with his mouth open, his face smooshed, his breathing deep and regular. I check his closet, under his bed, under his desk.

I'm convinced Carl is not in the room, but I still feel him close, maybe in the yard or parked on the street. I turn the flashlight off and sit on the floor, leaning against the wall. I listen to Jacob's breathing and for signs of Carl—a creaking floorboard, a cough in the darkness. I can't help but wonder what became of our fathers.

At school, on Monday after our date, I wait for Jocelyn to spread the news about me. I sit on the concrete next to P.F. during lunch and bum a smoke.

Jocelyn sits next to me, saying, "Move over, motherfucker," and pushes P.F. aside. It's the first time I've ever seen her sit down at lunch.

After school, she's waiting for me in the parking lot. I look down at her dusty green combat boots as we walk across the asphalt. She lights two cigarettes once we're in my car, and hands me one as we drive out of the lot. I keep waiting for her to ask questions or make some kind of statement. Something feels like it's about to happen.

We're a couple blocks from her house—our cigarettes half gone—when she says, "I read minds."

"What?" I stop the car in the middle of the road, my hands cold and sweaty on the wheel. I feel like my blood has cooled two degrees and reversed course.

She squints straight ahead through her smoke. "It's more like I get a picture in my mind and I know the other person's pain."

"What kind of picture?" I say, wondering what she's seen in my head.

A car behind me honks, and I start moving slowly.

"It's like I see what happened to them—not the facts, more like…the shape of the pain. It's knowing beyond words, know what I mean?"

"Yeah," I say, staring straight ahead. Yet, I don't know what she means. I don't know anything. I feel like I'm in a dream, flying a spaceship that I forgot how to operate.

"It used to freak me out," she says. "I thought I was cursed. I tried to get rid of it."

"Get rid of it how?"

She laughs. "How do you think?"

I think about how she's always pacing, cussing, getting piercings in her eyebrows, nose, tongue, and who knows where. The way she pops, drinks, or smokes anything that's handed to her.

When we get to her house, I park crooked in the driveway, blocking the sidewalk.

She flicks her cigarette out the window and rolls the glass up. "Then I figured it out," she says. "It's a gift. I can use it to help people."

She turns in her seat. "People I care about."

She leans toward me and I wonder if we're going to make out, but she just pecks me on the cheek. "See you tomorrow, motherfucker."

*   *   *

We start hanging out together, but the same thing keeps happening. I just stop. Sometimes Carl pops into my head. Sometimes he's there between us, or hovering in the corner of the room. Other times I just go blank. My mind empties and my body goes slack and I slip outside of time. Every time it happens, Jocelyn waits for me to come back. She lies next to me, her hand stroking my shoulder or my head.

The third time—one afternoon in Jocelyn's bedroom—Carl is at my back, speaking into my ear.

"*You're mine. You'll always be mine.*"

I roll away from Jocelyn and face the wall.

"*You really think she'd want you if she knew what you did?*"

"Sorry," I say.

"*Motherfucker,*" Jocelyn says, and it feels like she's talking to Carl.

*   *   *

No matter how much I cut, I can't get Carl out of me, can't stop feeling him in my life, wondering where he is or when he might come back.

I search Internet sites that sell information about people. They'll give you a tease for free and then want a credit card number for more. I type in Carl Randall and get a long list in various cities around the world. Of course he wouldn't use his own name, so I try some variations. Carlos Randolph. Randy Carlotta. More long lists, a few in Missouri and Illinois, but I know I'll never find him this way.

That night in bed I hear Carl whisper my name— *Daniel*—in my ear. I go to the computer and type in Jacob Daniel. It's creepy enough to make sense. The search returns forty-seven Jacob Daniels. I scroll down the list, clicking names in Omaha, Boise, and Des Moines. Then I see Topeka, a city big enough to hide in (close to St. Louis, but not too close—across state lines).

I sneak into my mom's room and take the billfold from her purse. Back in my room, I punch in her Visa number and soon have more info on Jacob Daniels of Topeka, Kansas, including his address (3607 Washington), age (41), marital status (single), profession (retail manager), and place of employment (Kleenmax Car Wash). There's no photo, but I'm positive it's Carl. I can feel it.

I print the profile and a map with directions, and go back to bed with the pages held tightly in my hand.

*   *   *

The next day I ask to borrow P.F.'s gun. I've seen the hunting trophies at his house, the animal heads on the walls, and photos of him posing with dead deer. After school, as we're driving in my car and smoking a spliff, I ask him, "Like…do you have a gun, or what?"

He nods, wheezing. "Three."

"Can I borrow one?"

"What for?"

I look over at him, not sure what to say. He's staring at me with his bloodshot blue eyes, his eyebrows raised in anticipation of my answer.

"I'd rather not say…if you don't mind."

He laughs and repeats my words back to me, exaggerating their formality. *"If you don't mind,"* he says. "I'd like to borrow your firearm for purposes of a personal nature, which I'd prefer not to disclose, *if you don't mind.*"

He laughs, and I laugh along with him, a stoned laughing fit.

After we quiet down I say, "So, is it cool?"

"Can you shoot?" he asks.

I shrug. I've lived in Missouri all my life, but none of my mom's boyfriends ever took me hunting.

"I'll loan you the .22," he says. "But you better not off yourself."

*   *   *

I'd be lying if I said I don't think about it, cutting deeper until I slice an artery. It's not that I want to kill myself, at least not most days. I just want to get rid of the Carl part of me—that tumor of evil poisoning my life. If I could kill that part and let the rest live, I would, but I know that's not possible. Some days I think about doing it anyway, killing the rest of me to get rid of the Carl part.

However, on this day—the day I ask to borrow P.F.'s gun—I have something else in mind.

Two weeks before Thanksgiving, P.F. and I drive to a field west of the city. It's a clear day, the sun warm on my face as morning fades into afternoon. He gives me a quick lesson on gun safety, loading, unloading, and working the safety, using the sight, pulling the trigger.

"This is basically a toy," P.F. says. "I mean...it'll kill a rabbit or whatever, but if you wanna hurt something big—you gotta get close."

"How close?"

"Like point blank."

He sets some Mountain Dew cans on a rock and we stand five car lengths away. When I pull the trigger the first time, the explosion and recoil surprise me, even though I'm prepared. My heart races. It feels like something real just happened, like I've just taken possession of a part of myself for the first time. Each time after that it feels the same way. Each shot is a line being drawn, a statement being made, a step being taken.

I take off my jacket and get serious. I imagine the can is Carl's face, then his crotch. My aim slightly improves.

Later, we pop some fresh Mountain Dews and sit on a rock to soak in some sun.

"So how are things with Jocelyn?" P.F. asks.

I shrug. "I'm still a virgin, if that's what you're asking."

"I didn't even know you were a virgin."

"I thought everyone knew," I say. Then, I realize that in a way I'm not a virgin. I don't know if I'm one or not. I don't know what I am.

I stand up, dizzy. The upper half of my body feels like it's being torn away from the lower part, my stomach wrenched. I throw up a stream of Mountain Dew and a half-digested ham and cheese sandwich in the dirt. I puke a few more times, then dry heave, leaning over with my hands on my knees. Afterward, my head throbs and a cold sweat covers my face. I walk to a nearby oak tree and sit in the shade, on a layer of crunchy leaves.

P.F. follows me and sits nearby. I wait for him to ask, "What the fuck was that? Are you okay?" Instead, he just hands me his Mountain Dew. I take a sip and try to rinse the foul taste out of my mouth.

*   *   *

The next week, I bring Jocelyn home to meet Jacob. She paces the rooms of my house like a cheetah in a cage, looking skinny in her jeans and army jacket, glancing at the family photos on the walls, but not for long enough to actually see them. She keeps turning around to look behind her, as if sensing a presence.

"It's cold as a motherfucker in here," she says, although the furnace blasts.

When we walk into the TV room, Jacob is slouched on the couch playing video games. He tosses the joystick aside as if to convince her he isn't a loser-gamer. He stands in the middle of the room in jeans and a red flannel shirt, his black hair half-covering his eyes, and stares at her like he wants to remember her later. I know that look, because it's the same way I looked at her the first time I saw her.

"Oh, my god!" she says. "You didn't tell me your brother was hot. How many girlfriends do you have?"

He shrugs. "A couple."

"You never said anything about any girlfriends," I say.

"Like I'd tell you." He scowls.

"Oh, but you'll tell some random girl you just met?"

He gazes at her, as if making one last effort to imprint her image into his brain for later reference.

"Don't stare," I say, "it's not polite."

Everything is great—my brother is impressed by my girlfriend, my girlfriend likes my brother. In my room it starts better than ever and I think: My turf, maybe that's what I needed! Then I think: This bed. It's the same bed.

I get up and walk across the room to get away from the feeling of Carl, but it doesn't help. I pick my guitar up and swing it at my lamp, knocking it onto the carpet. I bring the guitar down on it again and again, smashing the shade, shattering the bulb, and creating a broken kind of music that feels right. I kneel on the floor, pick up a piece of the broken bulb, and test its sharpness with my fingertip.

Jocelyn stands and watches.

"What happened?" Jacob asks, coming in the door.

I slice my left forearm with the bulb shard, instantly drawing blood.

"Stop it, freak!" Jacob kicks my thigh.

"Come on, babe," Jocelyn says, pulling him away.

I make another cut, parallel to the first.

"Make him stop!" Jacob says with tears and panic in his voice.

"That's not what he needs from us," she says, leading him out of the room.

A few minutes later she comes back in and shuts the door.

I'm on the floor, leaning against the dresser and gripping my left arm with my right hand. There's blood coming up between my fingers. My whole body is concentrated in a point of pain.

"Is he okay?" I ask.

She sits next to me and leans against the dresser.

"He's never seen me do it," I say.

Still, she doesn't say anything. I don't know what her silence means. Is it judgment or something else? Knowing beyond words?

"It's cool if you wanna, like, go hang with someone else," I say.

I feel her staring at my face, but I don't meet her gaze.

She pulls my hand away from my arm and holds it in her own, getting my blood on her palm and between her fingers. She leans over and kisses my sliced-up arm once, twice, three times. Then, she runs her pierced and studded tongue across my wounds.

*   *   *

On Thanksgiving it's just the three of us—me, Jacob, and my mom. I spend all morning helping my mom make a huge dinner. There's a final feeling about everything. Tomorrow, I'll drive to Topeka and shoot Carl in the face or the balls—or both. I'm not sure what I'll do afterwards. Maybe I'll do a Cobain, or maybe I'll just let them throw me in jail. Either way, nothing will be the same. Still, I'm strangely calm and happy. Carl will no longer have the power to haunt me or bring his evil back into my life, or into Jacob's life.

My mom keeps saying how "nice" it is that I'm helping her, how "nice" to have me around. The weird thing is, I agree. It *is* nice—nice to smell the food and help mash the potatoes, baste the turkey, nice to hear the sound of warfare coming from the other room, where Jacob is playing Call of Duty.

I'm chopping celery for the dressing and my mom comes over and hugs me. She's gained a few pounds and the hug is soft. "I'm so proud of you," she says.

For a second I have doubts about my plan. What I'm about to do will bring a whole new level of pain to her and Jacob, but I know it's the only way to remove Carl from our world—mine and Jacob's.

*   *   *

At two AM I'm on the 70 West doing sixty-five and drinking Red Bulls to stay alert. I grip the wheel, my whole body tight and bunched up. I breathe in, I breathe out. There's a fist-sized rock at the center of my chest where my heart should be. I keep turning the heat up and down. It's a cold November night outside, but in the car I'm sweating and shivering at random.

I try to clear my mind, but what keeps coming back is my mom hugging me and saying, "I'm so proud of you."

I turn the stereo on. There's a cheesy up-tempo song about love playing. "Happy Together"

I think of Jocelyn and start to panic, gasping for air and gripping the wheel tighter. I turn the radio off.

The road is nearly vacant. I pass through a tunnel of blackness—vast stretches of unlit plains and farmlands on either side, an occasional exit with filling stations and truck-stop diners. The signs tell me I'm getting closer to Topeka, but on the empty roads I wonder if I'm still in the world, if I still exist, if I was ever here.

I keep one eye on the speedometer because my brain can't tell how fast I'm going. It's the fatigue, or the Red

Bulls, or the adrenaline, or all of it mixing together. My ears are ringing and I keep thinking that it's all about to end. The plains give way to more buildings, exits with Denny's and Shell signs. I cross the Kansas River and think *Rubicon*.

I take my exit and wind my way through mostly deserted streets. A cop sits in his car in a Starbucks parking lot. It hits me that I could be on *COPS*—a strung-out teen with a loaded rifle that's wrapped in a quilt in the backseat. I drive by slowly, staring straight ahead.

Dawn is just starting to break as I leave the main streets and enter the heart of the neighborhood, with stop signs on nearly every corner. It's a poor area with fenced-in yards, littered with children's bikes, wagons, skateboards, Big Wheels. Most of the houses are small and don't have garages. Both sides of the streets are lined with faded economy cars, run-down pickups, dented vans.

The house at 3607 Washington is small and gray, or maybe dark blue—it's hard to tell in the dim light. I park across the street. When I stop the engine, my ears roar like there's a raging river in my brain. My heart is pounding, my shirt is soaked with cold sweat under my jacket, and I'm breathing hard. I start to pee, but stop it.

I'm gripping the steering wheel and can't seem to let go, even though my brain is trying to tell my hands to loosen their grip. Carl is on the other side of that door, enclosed in a thin layer of lumber, sheet rock, and insulation.

I know I need to act fast. It's getting lighter and if I don't move soon I'll lose the element of surprise—or chicken out. I detach my fingers from the wheel and reach into the backseat. I cradle the gun in its blanket like an oddly shaped baby, take three breaths, and think of Jacob lying in his bed. When I open the car door, a blast of cold air hits me. I walk across the street, my boots crunching and scraping against the cold asphalt. The sounds of morning birds compete with the whooshing of blood in my ears.

There's a chain link fence around the yard. I open the gate by lifting a lever. As I close it behind me, it occurs how bizarrely civilized I'm being. Why not just kick it down, or better yet shoot my way through it?

I climb the three steps to the door and stand on a black doormat that says "Welcome" in white block letters. I knock lightly and then ring the bell. I step back, drop the blanket, and cock the gun like P.F. showed me. I point it at the door, my finger on the trigger. My heartbeats shake my whole body. I'm shivering and trembling.

The door opens and an old man in a blue flannel robe stares at me. He's got a cane in one hand and an oxygen tank on wheels next to him. There's a tube going from the tank to his nose. The skin on his face and hands is dry, yellow, and papery—dotted with dark splotches.

"Where is he?" I ask.

"What's gotten into your head, son?" he says.

"Where's Carl? I know he's here."

"Come now, stop this nonsense." The old guy takes a step forward and holds out his hand, seemingly unafraid of death.

I push past him and into the house. It's hot—heat pumping through the vents—and it stinks like piss and garbage. It's hard to breath; my eyes fog. The living room is chaotic—dirty dishes on the table, blankets on the couch, and papers on the floor. I move down the hall. In the first bedroom is an unmade bed. I can tell by the smell that it's the old man's room. The other bedroom is neat. The bed is stripped, the closet bare, the dresser drawers empty. If it's Carl's room, he hasn't lived here in a long time.

"Fuck!" I shout.

I stand there and try to think. I pull the printout from my pocket and try to read it. The room is too dark, my mind too jumpy.

It hits me that I'm standing in a stranger's house in Topeka with a gun.

I rush back through the house. The kitchen if filthy, piles of dishes on the counter and in the sink. One part of the counter is covered with pill bottles. I pick one up and look at the label: *George Jenkins*.

Not Jacob Daniels, not Carl Randall. Not even close.

Carl is not here. Never was. Not even Jacob Daniels.

I walk back to the front door. The old man is on the porch with his cane and green tank. He seems to be peering up at the dawn-pink sky, his head cocked, listening to something.

I walk around so that I'm standing in front of him, my shaky legs spread for support, the gun pointed at his face. "Where the fuck is he? Tell me right now you old fucker."

"What's troubling your heart, son?"

"Shut up and tell me. Why isn't he here? Why did he do this to me?"

"Folks don't always do what's right," the old guy says. "We are all depraved by nature."

"I can't live with this." I'm walking in place, stepping on one foot, then the other, the sight of the gun sweeping back and forth across the man's wrinkled face, now blurry through my tears.

"He ruined my life."

"We all stand in need of salvation," he says.

"I don't know what the fuck you're talking about."

"There's time for you yet."

I shake my head. "There's no time. I'm fucked. He *fucked* me."

I take a couple of steps back. My feet get caught in the blanket. As I fall backward, the gun goes off and a nearby tree explodes, spewing dozens of blackbirds into the clear blue sky.

*   *   *

I'm on my back looking up into the face of an old man with blue eyes.

"Rest easy, son," he says.

"I'm not—" I start, but I can't finish because of my throbbing head.

"You took a tumble…best not to move."

I sit up and puke a stream of Red Bull on the quilt, which is now draped over my body.

"Help is on the way," the man says. "I phoned the emergency folks."

I puke until I'm dry heaving, a sharp pain in the middle of my head and a dull throb in the back.

Emergency folks include cops. I stand up, dizzy, nauseous, looking around. "Where's the—?"

"My conscience won't allow me to return your firearm," he says, "in your state."

My state? What's my state? Missouri, Illinois or Kansas? Living or dead?

I hear a siren in the distance. I stagger down the path, leaning forward to ease the pain in my head. I pass through the gate, close it behind me, and replace the latch.

People have come out of their houses in robes and sweat suits. They stand watching me. I get in the car and start the engine. I look back and the old man is still standing there, leaning on his cane. There's a tuft of white hair on his head, like a sputtering white flame or a weak halo. He looks like a being from another world—an alien or angel who's unaffected by humans and their stupid, crazy ways.

I drive away, winding through the streets of Topeka, single family homes on wide streets lined with large trees. It looks just like my town, and I realize I could be anywhere, anywhere U.S.A.—where each house contains a monster or an angel. You never know what you'll get until you knock on the door.

The sun is up now. It's bright in my eyes and I have no shades. I'm hot and cold, sweating and shivering, still feeling sick in my stomach. People are walking their dogs and gathering newspapers off their front steps, living normal lives. I keep driving until I'm in a zone of strip malls, gas stations, a Dairy Queen, and a McDonald's.

I find myself in an industrial park, a warehouse district. Large semis stand idle at loading docks, vast parking lots empty of cars. I pull into a lot and stop in the middle, careful to park within the lines for some strange reason. Again, the roar is in my ears when I stop the car. I pull the profile of Jacob Daniels from my pocket. The print swims in front of my eyes, unreadable. Why did I ever think it held an answer to my problems? Why did I think I could protect Jacob from the evil in the world? Why did I think I could fix myself by shooting someone, even Carl?

I reach under the dash to my secret compartment and find my emergency spare X-ACTO. I pull up the sleeve of my jacket, carve a new line—feel the familiar sting. Blood seeps from beneath the skin. I cut deeper. Blood drips onto my jeans.

I lean my head against the steering wheel. My throat is making sounds I've never heard before, wounded animal noises.

I dare myself to keep going, dig and slice until I hit the artery.

I try to think of Carl, to hear his voice, to feel his presence in my life pushing me toward revenge in self-death. Instead, I see that old man in his blue robe with his wisp of white hair.

"There's time for you yet. Rest easy, son."

HeLa, HeLa
Jess Gulbranson

If you could bring someone back from the dead—just one—who would the absolute worst choice be?

We asked that question one day in the cafeteria, and there were plenty of answers.

"Jack the Ripper..." offered Ruby the anesthetist.

Almost immediately Randy piped up with a grip of names. "Hitler? Walt Disney? Tupac and Biggie?" He gave me an apologetic look, adjusting the safety goggles he'd absent-mindedly left on his forehead.

"Jesus Christ," Scott responded with expected deadpan from the next table over.

"Scott, of course you would say that," said Ruby.

He always shared our conversations, but never sat

with us. That's just how he was.

"How about you, Sharon?"

"Don't mind me, I'm just black." Snarky, but I couldn't really answer the question. The thought of my father briefly entered my mind. However, I didn't want to mention him out loud. The motherfucker deserved the medical waste cremains that he had become.

There were a few more suggestions, but none I remembered when this whole conversation came back to me. It's strange, but it was only when I was alone that I wondered whether the converse was as interesting— obviously not; it never came up. My mother? My grandmother? Beyond that I didn't know much about my family until later, when I started digging out of curiosity. A few more jumps up the matriarchal tree, and look who I found. Her name was Henrietta, and she was…unique.

This was an amazing find. How had I never heard of her? When I was a little girl, there'd been a couple of people in the family of whom we never talked. I figured it was because we were even dirtier poor in the olden days. Even so, it never made sense as an adolescent, and became a non-issue when I went back east on a scholarship when I was fifteen. By the time I finished school and murdered my father, I didn't have much reason to go home, and all the immediate family had dwindled to just my grandmother. When she passed I was alone.

In all my time studying biochemistry, the strangest thing was that my celebrated forebear never came up — no fawning professors or curious dorm lurkers. Why? It seemed that fifty years ago (or so) a book had been written about her. There was a surge in public interest about Henrietta's story—and biomedical ethics in general—but by the time 2020 or so had rolled around, she disappeared. Not just from the fickle reading public, which would be expected, but from everything. The more I dug, the more it seemed that someone had tried to bury this story. Not that it was hard these days—as the flow of information back then had been much more promiscuous.

It made sense at the time—people are morbid, and we love to hear about gore and guts and revel in other people's misery. In Henrietta's case, it went beyond morbid. It kicked over into *abomination*, if you looked at it a certain way. Twenty years or so after she died (when the Johns Hopkins boys told her husband that they had some of Henrietta's cells) he didn't understand what they meant. That ignorant nigger—my great-great-grandfather, I guess—thought that they had his wife locked up in a cell, or something, and were doing experiments on her. The shadow of Tuskegee still loomed pretty large in those days.

Whatever the reason, the story of Henrietta disappeared. I read everything I could, and re-read it—old books on break in the cafeteria, or in the lab waiting for something to cook, e-books on my phone in the bathroom, and in bed while Jennifer tossed and turned next to me. It was all I thought about, and I'm not even sure why, other than the simple fact that I get like that. Jennifer and I broke up somewhere in there, and I was so bad I hardly noticed that she was gone. Until finally the obsession drained out of me like a lanced boil. Everything felt clear all of a sudden. At the time I couldn't tell whether I had burned some wisdom into some deep part of my mind, or simply let go of the issue as being too weird, too dark, too painful.

At first, nothing about my worldview had changed. Everything was going to shit faster than our organic toga-and-jetpack dreams could be realized—sectarian violence on the streets, facile drones in the workplace, a constant hum and whine of half-realized wireless infrastructure. I got back with Jennifer, and the makeup sex was rough and wonderful. I was a research biochemist, which was as close to being a rock star in these days of Big Pharma as a black girl could expect. Didn't she realize the stresses I had been under? Regardless we were back together, and that night I found myself again laying sweating, on top of the covers with Jennifer knocked out beside me, unable to sleep in the dim half-light of the phones and pads and screens that gave off their dormant glow throughout the room.

Henrietta had been to the moon. She had stood in the blast of a nuclear weapon. She had helped—if some research was to be believed—to perpetuate the Cold War another decade and a half. But what had I done? Where had I been?

Back at work, I slipped into a comfortable rhythm. My coworkers (facile drones) were content to let me be the introvert I normally was, the intensity of the previous months gone. One day in the cafeteria—looking at Scott with his esoteric light reading, oblivious to human nicety—I realized just how close I'd been to…well, becoming him. A lifetime of avoiding eye contact, of laughing at jokes that no one else was smart enough to get—*Wow!*—I felt, almost blessed.

This kept up for a while and, in moments of stark

desperation when the lights were low, I felt as if there was something I missed, something I should be doing. This comfortable shell wasn't me, and maybe there was no me. How was it that the people closest to me couldn't see that? This time I was the one who broke up with Jennifer. I told her I was fucking someone else—a guy, ten guys, her mom—testing. She bought it, or was close enough for my purposes, and she was gone for good.

She couldn't even see through that. How the fuck could I expect her to help me figure this out? My existential questioning was becoming a crisis, and I knew that I didn't have the requisite background in literature to make that work. I needed help.

How was it that this crisis—that felt so keenly like vertigo in the back of the knees, and pit of the stomach— could go invisible to the people around me, when the episode of previous months had been so stark? I would get my answer, but it was just another nail in the coffin of meaning. There was no such thing as fate, things happened because…they happened. In this case they happened because a couple of geniuses—a couple of Scotts, so to speak—had been there before, broken trail for those of us trapped in our murky little existences.

James, a friend of mine from school (who'd ended up

in sociology and game theory instead of real science), got in touch to ask for a pair of eyes for what he was working on—my eyes, specifically. We'd always worked well together. He was a why-guy, and I was a how-girl, and since he was a faggot there was never any reason to worry. James was working on something for the eleventy-first, or whatever Congress of the Mind, dipping into redefining some of the categories of the Battery—yes, that Battery, the Huysman-Macmanus Battery. If you were a chimp, or a dolphin, or a lowish-to-midlevel artificial intelligence, you could thank Huysman and Macmanus for the fact that you could take a standardized test out of Kafka's wet dreams and—if you passed—get a driver's license, or be conscripted, or fuck someone over the age of consent.

It seemed that there was a huge body of research behind the famous duo's test. James had his ideas about why they framed the questions a certain way, but he wanted me to look into how it made sense. If anyone could be critical about the dirty legwork behind two of the most hyped scientists ever…well, it would be yours truly. The pay was right—Congress was rolling in it, thanks to some of its silicon-brained silent partners. It would be a nice diversion.

The first thing I did (well, aside from deleting all the messages Jennifer sent me) was to go straight to the sources—not the men themselves, no, they were dead. Macmanus was murdered under mysterious circumstances, and not long after that Huysman had walked out onto the Freedom Plaza, lit a match, and rode a Jerry can straight to that big testing facility in the sky— nothing like the first world problems of a couple of white dudes.

I went to the H-M Institute, where the two's work continued, and asked nicely. More specifically, I ended up wrist-deep in a very sweet, young research senior, and she let me into the archives.

There was only so much genetic sequencing and titration that I could do before I went completely batshit insane. Getting to delve into Macmanus's wartime journals, before the two started working together, and Huysman's papers from New Ingolstadt U—hell, they even had some of his poetry—was more like it. The Institute was nothing if not thorough. This was becoming a dream come true.

Yet, the more I read, the more I was convinced that something was missing. It wasn't just me, either, though it did seem a timely mirror of my internal conflict. Apart from their famous work on the Battery, these two had been into some weird shit that was more spelled out by what wasn't in the archives than what actually ended up on the page. On-and-off, Huysman had done work with some people named Sentinel and Osborn. From the few references I could see, they'd been researching ghosts and goblins, or something.

Macmanus's time with DARPA had yielded a great quantity of black ink—redacted this and classified that—but I was savvy enough to figure out that it was mind control and new school germ warfare (a tailored version of Ebola, its virulence and resilience finely tuned for maximum lethality). To top it all off, his team had figured out a way do some crazy horseshit with chelated manganese that let the little critter have extra-somatic memory. You know…like giving one of the world's worst viruses a fucking notepad, so it could remember all the genetic permutations that worked. Forget those pesky generations of trial-and-error evolution. I was jealous at how hardcore that was, how completely unique, but now it was buried under posterity, and popularity, and death.

I'd gotten a good picture of what drove these two to such heights of scientific achievement (it was the same alchemical lust that Newton had) and I was just about to call it a week, when one of the last things in the collection caught my eye, or, my ear. It was one of very few audio recordings that the two had done themselves, and I almost didn't continue listening to it—mainly because of their annoying accents: Macmanus's high and cloying Virginia drawl, and Huysman's vaguely Eastern European monotone. The recording was casual at first, as if they were a little reluctant to get to the point, dancing around something.

When it came out, I had to rewind and listen to it a couple of times. Even though I understood it in a perfectly logical way—the same way they presented it—there was a part of me that didn't really believe it. Why would something like this get hidden? I know now, but at the time it flustered me. When the talking was all done and the speakers started blaring a weird, overtone-feedback, I hastily shut the recording off. Maybe I didn't believe what it was all about, but some part of me was terrified. I had seen that movie with the cabin and the demons and the chainsaw.

I took the recording—just took it—and for good measure copied the recipe for Ebola Centralia. I stormed out, leaving the research senior with just a wink. I could smell her on my hand for two days. The wages of sin, I guess.

Huysman and Macmanus—those two magnificent bastards—had uncovered something incredible. After everything I had learned, I think at this point I knew less about the "why" of their work on human and inhuman sentience, but it was okay. The world was a gray, washed-out piece of shit, but I had stumbled on something special, something monumental—bringing the dead back to life.

Yes, not something that was part of polite conversation—outside of morbid university hospital cafeterias—but something I'm sure everyone thinks about more than often. Apparently, years and years before the Battery, when H & M had just started working together, they came upon the ruins of a cover-up that sent Roswell home with its tail between its legs. Like something out of a bad science fiction novel, there was a boy, a young man, who'd been able to call the dead back from the grave. Not like zombies, but more like the ghosts, or souls, or something.

The name Osborn once again cropped up. The parapsychologist was involved, and had been killed during what Macmanus continually referred to as "The Smithsonian Affair." When the affair concluded—with a lot of people dead and a significant number of anthropological treasures destroyed—it was all swept up by whatever part of the government dealt with this kind of thing, outside of bad fiction. In all of the alphabet soup, the Office of Naval Intelligence kept appearing, some horseshit about Potomac Jurisdiction. That's where Huysman and Macmanus had gotten whatever research was done on the boy. Before he was snuffed it ended up at DARPA, and then in Macmanus's hot little hands.

With the boy dead, the research was at a dead end. The only thing of substance had been a recording of some magnetic resonance this-and-that, which the two geniuses took to like D.J.'s sampling old vinyl, and shit out a masterpiece with help from the quantum gate computing that was then in its infancy. It was a practical (inasmuch as black magic could be 'practical') method of summoning the dead from wherever it was that the dead were. Their version didn't work exactly as the original. It took a body, or at least a convenient lump of biomass, and a human operator to collapse the audible resonance waveform. Jesus, listen to me, turning into a Scott.

They started with bugs, went to goats and pigs, and ended with...well, with something they wouldn't admit to on tape. All I could tell for sure—as sure as anything—

was that this resonance thing worked, or at least the smart guys believed it did, and I believed in them (which was odd, for me).

If I'd really been as self-aware as I thought, I might have seen exactly where I was going with this, but as I hope I've made clear I'm not much of a why girl. Maybe James could've helped me figure it out—if I hadn't made up some bullshit about Freemason Lodges and Catholic childhood abuse and black-bag military wet work, and then cut him out of my research entirely. He was not getting at my discovery. James was too limited a thinker. Maybe I was, too, but the wide scope of potential was opening in my rotten brain. Besides, he'd see the results soon enough.

I ended up at my lab. It was the only place I felt at home. I knew what I wanted to do, but couldn't admit it to myself. Pacing only seemed to be pushing me farther away from realization. I took a narrow Pyrex dish from a cabinet and set it on the counter. In the back of the lab was a glass-fronted cabinet of chemicals. I reached into the back, took out a brown jar, and brought it back to the counter. Then, I put on some rubber gloves.

The grooves on the cap had almost been worn smooth by how many times I opened and closed it. After pouring some of the clear liquid into the dish, I replaced the cap. I put two fingers into the dish and brought them to my face, rubbed the fingers together. There was a faint sour whiff from the substrate—Aflatoxin. If you took a big swig from the jar (not that there was a big swig left) you'd get throat cancer pretty quick, or esophageal cancer, which the sliding scale clinic would misdiagnose as acid reflux and hiatal hernia, before you died in agony a few months later, your throat liquefying so that you couldn't even scream anymore.

The same exact thing would happen if someone poured it into your morning cup of Luzianne every day for a week. Later, my father's cancer would be blamed on his smoking, which at that point was illegal. Fucking your daughter was illegal, too, but he had gone ahead with that anyway. All of us were twisted, rotten inside. It's just the way things were. You could understand someone who set themselves on fire, or who got shot in the face while trying to do underground research on fresh bodies, the spoils of a diamond conflict. It was a dirty world.

I looked at the liquid on my fingertips and wondered—what if I took those two fingers and inserted them in my cunt, all the way up to the cervix? Would my flesh inside turn purple and livid like Henrietta's did before they biopsied her and ushered in the age of modern medicine? Would I die quickly, like she did (ha ha), or would it dwell inside me like some satanic embryo? Jennifer had always wanted kids, and she always assumed I would be the one to carry them. She really didn't know me, at all. What if I did it, and called her up to tell her that we were expecting?

I realized I was gritting my teeth. I swept the Pyrex into the garbage, grabbed the bottle of Aflatoxin, and with one long look threw it in, as well—didn't need it anymore. I turned the glove inside out and flicked it away.

If you could bring someone back from the dead—just one—who would the absolute worst choice be? I was starting to understand the question, and allowing myself to think about the answer. Henrietta, my great-great grandmother, had been a giving, loving, generous woman. She had liked dancing and dressing sharp, despite her poverty, but she was dead. Though, that wasn't the end of it.

The cells from her cervical tumor (immortal, they called them—boy did they get that one right) were everywhere. The doctors at the time nicknamed the cell line "HeLa", a half-assed attempt to cover up their theft and marginalization of some poor, uneducated niggers. Almost every significant medical discovery had used these preternaturally hardy cells, and conservative estimates placed the level of contamination of all cell cultures in the world at ten percent, maybe twenty. Henrietta got around—she floated through the air, on lab instruments, in water supplies. Because of this, her cells were in every biomedical research facility, everywhere in the world. In the early parts of the millennium, it was calculated that Henrietta's cells had been cultured and multiplied so much that, all together, they would weigh in the *tons*. I tried to do the math as to how much would be around now—the calculations escaped me.

What would she do if she came back? She liked to dance and wear fine clothes. She was generous and giving. She filled medical waste depositories, and grew in large quantities on the Big Pharma space stations where they developed great new vaccines to be withheld from the third world. What would it look like when Henrietta looked back?

If you could bring someone back from the dead—just one—who would the absolute worst choice be? The world was a useless fucking waste and I was just a part of it, but I could stand apart, just once. Huysman, Macmanus, and Osborn, and all those nameless victims of "the Affair" had given me the clarity to understand that, had given me the means to do it.

I found the recording, loaded it up, and cranked the speakers. I fast-forwarded to the good part. I made my choice.

HeLa, HeLa.

Playing the Game
William Cook

There were five other guys sitting in the foyer—all
young, preppy, and clean cut—and then there's me, long
hair, old jeans, and half a beard, trying hard to shake off
the dregs of a hangover. I have an eight AM job
interview. One of those you think is just for you. You
turn up and a hundred other bums have all been told the
same story. The four other plebs and I checked the clock,
tick-tocking on the grey wall, eight-twenty AM. Ten
minutes earlier there were five of them, but one left. He
knew he wouldn't get the job, or maybe it was the old
crazy eyes I gave him, before he got up and walked out.

He quickly gave a copy of his embossed resume to the
dowdy receptionist, and asked her to pass it on to the

boss as he flew through the door, looking accusingly over his shoulder at me. I saw him through the window, giving me the bird and flapping his wordless preppy mouth, as he started his Mitsubishi or whatever it was. From that first retaliatory glance back over his shoulder, I had his face programmed. Christ, what a naïve dipshit. He didn't know me from Buddha. I could've been a bad ass gangbanger, a psycho-crazy serial killer, the dude that lived across the way and watched him and his young lovely say sweet nothings to each other in silhouette sadness, as they leave their house together — fuck him, he'd keep.

I leaned back and stretched my legs, put my hands behind my head and thought about the runners in the big race at noon—ten dollars on Slick in the first race, 12-1 odds, hot tip from old Charlie who worked the track religiously. After a day's racing Charlie would come down to the Fitzroy and pretend he was broke, trying to bum drinks off the other patrons, but I knew better since I used to see him at the track—usually at the counter stuffing wads of cash in his coat pockets, as he collected his takings. Charlie used to give me hot tips and free drinks to shut me up, but I wouldn't have told. I ain't a narc. I used to pay the old geezer with a few glasses of top shelf if his tips came in, which they usually did.

One of the students farted—a squelch noise, like he was trying to hold it in—his face went red, and everyone just looked the other way in disgust. They were all university students or graduates. I'd heard their banal conversations come fading in and out.

"So…you doing law? Oh yeah, me too"

"Hey, what's your major?"

One of them was asking me a question. I gave him an incredulous look and was just about to pluck something from the air, when I thought better of it. I folded my arms across my chest and rolled my eyes in the back of my thumping skull. He looked confused and turned back to his new pal. Fuck, the world's turned upside down, I thought. They're overqualified and wet behind the ears – reduced to dipping their heads below the surface to pay for their ticket out, after exhausting all their other funds.

I yawned and considered leaving, but it was warm and I had to wait around until midday for the first race. I looked out the office windows across the plant yard, semi-trailers weaving between the chemical reservoirs and production buildings. The yard must've been ten football fields in length.

"Wallace? Henry Wallace?" the plump receptionist called, then ushered me into the boss's office, her ample bosom heaving with the exertion of getting out of her too-small chair.

"Hello, Henry, my name's Reg" he said, as he reached over and shook my hand without getting up. He wore a denim shirt with the company logo emblazoned across the chest pocket, a Pall-Mall burning in an ashtray on his veneer desk.

"Have you ever done process work before?"

"Sure," I said.

"Can you work overtime, and are you okay working with toxic chemicals?"

"Yes and yes," I said.

"When can you start?" asked Reg.

"When do you want me to start?" I replied.

*   *   *

I left the office with a spring in my step. The sun was warm on my face. Despite a crisp breeze, everything seemed very clear and sharp. The sky was blue behind the cold, black clouds. I could taste all those wonderful beverages, unaffordable for too long—only begged for, which is so undignified, really. Ooohhh…those sweet warm whiskies, beautiful mad bourbon like an old lover come home, that devilish musky taste. No more betting on the nags for booze money now, things were looking up in the whole mad scheme of things here and now.

Gin, Bombay sapphire blue poetry in a bottle, must've been made of crystal Christ's tears for me now. I hadn't worked for three months and the money had dried up. A little bit of dope sold here and there bought my beer-bloating, kidney-killing booze. Man, was I sick of cheap wine and port. The dole paid the rent, but shit, I was one bored and beat motherfucker. The shakes took away reading, time kept ticking off itself, and doors kept getting knocked upon. There was a snatch of music here and there, the odd ceremony of intoxication via cheap wine and jagged dreams, mythologizing my existence with each measure of a cheap cup of wooden tea—a spliff to take the day away, cigarette the air into the ether, and now, liberation.

It's not true that all we downtrodden fellas don't want the work. Shit, if we're trying to go on the straight and straight, you can't live without it. If you want to live, and keep going and going headlong into inevitable death and stormy future, the destitute night begs you to have a job. You can't go bush—there's no escaping it. You want to escape, you have to work. No man can live without wheels in this crazy time of oppression, oppression, oppression. Besides, the plant was only six blocks away with a bar, a brothel, and a bottle-store between.

Shit! I didn't need any death-trap wagon wheels to statisticize my ass—I had everything I needed within stumbling distance. I had it made, man. I went to the track and, sure enough, old Charlie came through for me. Feeling good after scoring work, I put twenty down to win. Slick ended up paying, ten to one. Two hundred up, I headed for the Fitzroy, looking for Charlie.

"Top shelf tonight, Charlie. Top shelf for me, you, and I."

Things were looking up. I wasn't afraid. I know the laws of physics, man.

*   *   *

The first day at the plant was a drag, like all the other first days. The foreman—who in this case was an ugly, short bastard with a face like a cane toad—would inadvertently pair you up with a begrudging co-worker to be, who would usually instruct you to go get a coffee and keep out of the way, as you watch the heavenly interesting blue-collar action of the everyman. Well, I couldn't be but blue collar. It was ingrained from birth into my beaten brain, and every gene ached with the weight of downtrodden forefathers. Here I was stuck in the talon plant, with a huge Polynesian/German guy called Karl, who had biceps like big chocolate bowling balls. He didn't say much, which didn't bother me (in fact it suited me fine).

He showed me what to do, for I later found out that the poor bastard had been doing it for thirteen years. It took me an hour to get it down pat. The plastic buckets would be placed on the rollers. Take one, place it on the scales—the always grinding throb of the vat mixer making the poison, spittin' it out lickety-split, real quick. Take it off and hit the overhead chute button—red and big enough not to miss with a cross-eyed Monday morning hangover, the rat poison pellets dropped into the bucket with a sick thudding clatter, like dead sparrows falling on a tin roof. You hit the switch again at the cut-off weight, move full poisoned bucket to the left with a jerk, and repeat the process, waiting for a gap in time as the hopper mixed the poison and the talon, and hammered the plastic lids home with a rubber mallet. The trick was to stay ahead of the machine—no fuck ups, no lost time, just get the rhythm.

Pretty soon I got the rhythm, and could dream of my lovely mistress Ambrosia and her wonderful alluring forms and tastes. Oh, sweet delight, I would savor you for lost time in three nights, payday. Oh, yes—we have risen, born again. The always grinding throb of the vat mixer making the poison, spittin' it out lickety-split, real quick, kept chugging away into the knock-off hour. Karl, the dude with the bowling ball biceps and lips like stacked tires, kept my skinny beat white ass in line with his constant mixtures—stoking the hopper with fresh mix, horse abattoir by-product, don't you know? I packed the product. The smell was always deep, like musky wax, like burning soap. The stereo blasted reggae over the churn and mechanical chug, and hum, and thud of the hopper. Oh yeah, here it comes. I'm rolling home now.

*   *   *

After a few days you get into the swing of things. Your thinking gets freed up as you become the machine. The thoughts are like freight trains. They just keep coming, blasting through with profundity. Hell, man, the answers to the universe are propositioned, resolved, and resolutely dissolved again into the chemical ether of the factory floor, and the weekend's absolutions and intoxications. Smoko would roll around soon enough, the morning dissolved as we all filed languidly into the vast cafeteria, the machines still churning in our brains. The day's end would drift around soon thereafter. I pulled off my blue overalls, work boots, gloves, and threw them with inevitable, building disdain into my locker.

Standing outside the big barbwired gate, I lit a smoke and felt another eighty bucks of day's wage better off. Ten minutes later I had the knives on the stove, a nice fat sativa bud chopped into succulent spots on the chopping board, a bourbon rocks sitting on the bench. Ann came home and wrapped her lovely brown arms around my neck. I gave her a long, slow purple smoke spot. Knives hot, twisting every snake coil breath of smoke out of it. We kissed in warm, hard passion and made love for dinner. I slept so verily deeply, despite knowing I had to entertain the succubus of fitful employment in six hours.

*   *   *

Payday rolled around quickly, cashed up and hungry for action and relaxation in that order. Everybody shuffled into the cafeteria. The company subsidized the booze— flagons of draught beer or dry white wine. I slapped my five bucks on the counter and grabbed the wine. Five bucks...I couldn't believe my luck! I only ended up drinking six glasses, stood up to go to the bathroom, and fell back into the chairs and tables behind me. My legs were gone. I was good and drunk on six glasses!

Karl, the Samoan Schwarzenegger, laughed and raised his glass. "Comes a bit cheaper here, don't it, bro?"

"Wadd'ya mean?" I slurred.

"It's da chems, man—they build up in yo' blood. Don' worry, you get used to dem and its cheap piss, man!"

He leaned back on his chair and let rip a raucous laugh, as I excused myself and stumbled to the pissoir— my head spinning, legs rubbery. I put one hand out against the cold top of the steel urinal, and proceeded to drain my full bladder. I blinked my eyes and again looked. Shit—my piss-stream was a fluorescent green color! It fucking glowed in the dark.

Chriiissstt!

I stumbled out the gate and pointed my body toward the apartment. The pub rolled up quickly. Dodging cars full of curses, across the busy afternoon road, I went inside and sat down...

"Ya' can't sit there, mate," said the old, toothless geezer in the next booth.

"Yah, that's Tom's spot," his old buddy next to him chimed in.

"I don't see anybody sitting here. Where the fuck is the old bastard then?"

Everyone in the bar stopped talking and stared daggers in my direction. The huckory hag of a barmaid turned the rugby on the radio down. The old fart with no teeth pointed a skeletal finger at the wall behind the bench seat I'd attempted to claim. The plaque read:

TOM DOWNEY SAT HERE 1908–1986,
TRAGICALLY TAKEN FROM US
WHILE HEROICALLY RESCUING
A YOUNG CHILD FROM DROWNING
IN CLAYTON'S CREEK.
R.I.P. TOM
WE'LL SAVE YOU A SEAT, BUDDY!

I gave up, sighed, and shrank into my beer on a stool at the bar. Brilliant, my first drink at the local and they were already prepared to ban and string me up.

The barmaid turned up the rugby on the radio again, giving me a disgusted look...

...my hands and knees were bloody and raw, I could barely see, let alone walk, but I somehow made it home, exhausted and blind-drunk—no one home at eight PM on a Friday. Ann and the others must've gone out. I stripped all my clothes off and fell into bed, the chemicals and booze swimming in my battered brain. I woke up hunched over the toilet, bare white, hairy ass up in the air, vomit churning, body heaving, just as Ann and her mates rocked through the front door, which happened to be directly opposite the wide open bathroom.

Hey, come on in: *Welcome to the Show!*

* * *

The hangover lasted until Sunday night—enough time to eat a meal, apologize to Ann, and then make up. I rolled and lit a cigarette, and passed it to her. She stuck it between her full, succulent lips and took a drag. I lit up, inhaled and exhaled, sighing at the same time. I could feel her smooth, long legs under the sheets.

"So how's the job hunting goin', babe?" I asked her.

"There's nothing out there at the moment," she replied.

She took another drag, blowing the blue smoke into the shadows past the lamplight. I watched the smoke curl lazily upon itself, and then dissipate in the stale air hanging over the bed. She stubbed her smoke out in the glass ashtray beside the bed and turned her back to me, as she fell asleep.

I took another drag and watched the blue smoke twist into another swirl, like an eye (the eye of God, maybe?). I looked at her dyed blonde hair for a few minutes. She looked like a crumpled blanket. I rubbed my eyes and looked around the room—a few pieces of clothing, an alarm clock, shoes, half a bottle of scotch, and a duffel bag. I took another drag on my cigarette, breathing in deeply, trying to purge the stench of decay that permeated the room.

I slowly got out of bed and put on my clothes and shoes. I unplugged the clock and placed it, along with half of the scotch, in the bag. I opened the door, thinking about the runners in the first race tomorrow—one hundred dollars on Sure Thing in the second, 16-1 odds—another hot tip from old Charlie, who worked the track religiously.

The Fall of Nil
Sam D. Church II

The light shines into my eyes and I wake up for what feels like the first time. At first I am disoriented—the way you are after waking up from sleeping over at a friend's house as a kid. The only difference is that this is the house that I grew up in, in my room, and everything is the way I left it. I'm used to waking up in unfamiliar places—couches of people I just met at the bar the night before, in the tube slide at random playgrounds, in recycle bins, under bridges, or anywhere else where we can get shelter from the cold nights. I try to not stay with my parents unless it is absolutely essential.

My puppy, my baby, Rukus is curled up to my leg. When he sees that my eyes are open, he nonchalantly crawls over, with his belly hugging the sheets, and sticks his cold nose in my face to kiss me good morning. I am awake.

I walk down the stairs with Rukus weaving a figure eight between my legs the whole way. As I descend, the increasing aroma of my mom's cooking begins to seep in through my nostrils. I get to the bottom and the first thing my mom does is ask how I slept.

Then, my dad breaks in. "Good morning Rip van Winkle. You'd think that you haven't slept in two days."

Try four—and it's only two o'clock.

My mom turns around the conversation. "So, I kept some soup warm for you, and there are sandwiches in the fridge."

I pour myself a bowl of soup and grab two sandwiches. I also pour a bowl of puppy chow, which my parents have kept on reserve since I got Rukus. When I sit down my dad asks me what I've been up to, and I tell him that he doesn't want to know. He asks me how things are going with Jess, and I say that I don't want to tell him.

He bites back. "Well, I think I want to tell you something."

Then, it starts.

"I want you to look at that wall right there." He points at the wall to the left of me—the one with my brother's diploma. I know where this is going and really don't need to hear anymore.

He continues. "Notice that every other wall in this dining room is covered with pictures of our family…except that wall. That's because *that* wall is where we put Rick's high school diploma and, as much as we love the people on those walls, to put their picture next to his diploma would be like putting a nudie magazine next to the bible."

"What about Playboy? They're pretty classy." I had to say it.

He pretends not to hear anything and goes on. "That diploma represents the moment your mother and I could say that we've done our jobs as parents. That was when we could say he is ready to leave home if he so chooses. Then, he moved to Calgary and got his Bachelor of Commerce degree. He's now clearing six figures a year."

He pauses to see if I'm paying attention. "I don't think we've done our jobs with you, yet. I want you to stay here. You can upgrade and still graduate. It's freezing out there, and the streets are no place for a dog."

This is nothing I haven't heard before.

Changing tone, he says, "I am asking you, John, to stay with us."

"The name's not John! It's Nil!" I grab my guitar and my jacket, and take another sandwich for the road. "Thanks mom!"

I slam the door and Rukus and I are once again on our own. As we walk down the street, the fresh, sticky snow clings to us. There hasn't been snow like this in Vancouver for some time. The wet, brownish-white slush splashes up to my knees. We walk like this all the way to our regular spot at East Hastings Street. When we arrive, everyone is there—Brock, Spunk, and Mitch and Jess are sitting together on the bench, all drinking Colt 45's.

Once closer I can see that Mitch and Jess are holding hands. This, I wasn't expecting. Jess and I broke up less than two weeks ago, and this rat bastard—my best *friend*—wasted no time in taking her. I sit next to Jess and ask if Mitch if I can get a sip of his beer.

"Sure little fella," he condescends. "All you gotta do is pry it from my cold dead hands."

I can't believe it. The guy steals my girlfriend and won't even give me a little sip of his cheap malt liquor. I look at Jess and she directs her attention to the ground.

Brock and Spunk didn't acknowledge me when I said "hi". They just continue their conversation about how they're going to save the world. It sure is cold outside today.

There's a bag beside Mitch's leg. I ask what's in it.

He pulls out a bowling trophy for some guy named Jim Mitchell. I ask what he's doing with it, and he says that there's a guy who will give him two points of crystal meth for it.

I tell him I don't believe him.

He says he'll prove it.

Mitch polishes the rest of his Colt 45 off, kisses my ex-girlfriend, and then takes me to go see this guy. Rukus comes with us. I don't even attach his leash—he never likes to be more than two meters away from me, anyway.

We journey to this guy's place and its' huge. We walk up to his double doors and knock. The man that opens the door is unshaven, with bed hair and a piece of food above his lip, which neither of us mentions to him. He's wearing a pair of boxer shorts with prints of kissing lips all over them, a housecoat, and mismatched socks.

The man points his chin at me. "Hey, Mitch...who's this guy? What's he doin' here?"

"Forget about this guy, man. It's just Nil."

"Hey dude. Name's Champ." He slaps me on the shoulder and invites us in, taking the trophy from Mitch. As he does this, he shakes Mitch's hand and leaves a little baggy in his palm.

It is true.

I just have to ask why he is giving Mitch meth for this trophy. "Do you have a bowling fetish or what?"

Champ answers. "I don't just got bowling trophies, dude."

Then, he offers to show me the collection.

We walk past the pool table, the Jacuzzi, and the fifty-two inch plasma television, all the way to the trophy room. Some people collect exotic beer bottles, or comics, or stamps. Champ has a room full of other peoples' greatest accomplishments. Trophies cover the floor from all different sports, all different age groups, and all with different names. The walls are adorned with war metals and plaques that say things like *"Top Sales for 2001"* and *"Excellence in Grade Six Science"*. I see credentials for psychology, dermatology, criminology, and almost any other "ology" you can think of. There is a designated spot for high school diplomas.

I ask if he would give me two points for a high school diploma.

"You bet your ass, dude," he says as he lights a cigarette.

He exhales. "The more the merrier. Anytime one of my friends busts a joke about me not getting my high school diploma, I just show them this room, and remind them that I got enough diplomas as it is."

As we're walking back Mitch says, "Hey Nil, about Jess…"

I look at him, expecting an apology.

"Thanks for keeping her warm for me," he says as he punches me in the arm. Here is my best friend, whom I have forgiven time and time again, whom I forgave when I blacked out at a party, he took the couch I was sleeping on, and put me on the meridian of a busy road. I forgave him when he shot me in the ass with a pellet gun and made thirty-four cents doing it. I even forgave him when he pissed on me while I was sleeping. I choke on my own words and rub my sore arm. I can forgive this, too.

When we get back to the spot, the meth is finished within a few hours. Within an hour after that, I crave more. I think about my father rubbing that diploma of Rick's in my face. Meanwhile, the craving starts clawing at me from the inside, like the paw of a bobcat. Then, I remember that it's Friday, and Friday is movie night for my parents. They won't be at home between eight and ten.

I ask Jess what time it is. She says it's seven-thirty. So I take Rukus and we're off to my parents' house. As I walk away, Mitch asks where I'm going. I tell him that I'm off to get a high school diploma for Champ.

"Well we're coming with." He runs up beside me and playfully puts me in a headlock. The others eventually trail along.

It was supposed to be in and out. I have the key, so I could just walk in, take the diploma off the wall, and then leave. As soon as we get in, Spunk sits down on my dad's chair and turns on the television, Brock goes to see what's in the fridge, and Mitch runs upstairs. I'm already starting to regret this idea, but I keep my mind on the task at hand and go straight to the diploma.

When I have it in my hand, I get right back to the front door and try to round up the troupe. By this time, Spunk is fishing through my parent's DVD's and taking what he likes, Brock is heating up the leftovers of my mom's soup, and Jess had followed Mitch upstairs for reasons that I would rather not know.

I run upstairs and my parents' bedroom door is locked. I bang on the door. "Come on guys. We gotta go!"

There is no response, just some mild moaning. I continue banging on the door for a couple of minutes before I give up.

I get back downstairs and Spunk is now going through my parents' CD's. Next to him is a recycling bag, containing all the DVD's he picked. Brock has taken Spunk's place on my dad's chair. He's eating an overflowing bowl of soup. The soup is splashing all over the chair and carpet.

"Seriously, guys, this isn't funny," I say, but my pleas fall on deaf ears.

I patiently stand by the door, until Mitch and Jess finally come downstairs. Jess is wearing bracelets that cover both arms, rings on all of her fingers, and several necklaces around her neck.

Mitch says something that is a great relief. "Come on, guys. Let's get the hell out of here."

On Mitch's demand, Spunk throws what CD's he's holding in the bag. Brock drops half a bowlful of soup on the floor. Mitch picks up the bowl, and we walk to the back door in the kitchen. Before we exit Mitch throws the bowl through the window, which shatters into a million little pieces.

"What was that all about?" I point at the broken window.

He gives his outrageous reply. "Well I was looking out for you little fella." He messes up my hair. "If no windows were broken your parents would've known you used your key to get in." With that he walks out the door.

"They will be able to tell that you broke the glass from the inside."

He shrugs.

I follow him. The bowl lying in the back yard is surrounded by shards of glass. As I shut the door, I look into the house one last time. My mom walks in through the front door. She looks right at me for a cold hard second, and then immediately looks at the ground as to pretend she doesn't see me.

We walk back to the spot. During the walk, that brief moment where my mom saw me lingers in the back of my head. I wonder if she told my dad. I doubt she had to. It's more than obvious that I'm responsible for what happened.

When we get to the spot, Mitch asks me if he could see the diploma, so I pass it to him. He takes the diploma and hands it to Jess. With the diploma safely in Jess's hand, he smirks and punches me square in the nose. I fall like a ton of bricks, and as I fall, I look at the hand that Mitch punched me with and see that he's wearing my dad's class ring. I feel a warm, damp drip running down to my lips as I lie face up in the snow. I lick my lip and taste my own blood. Mitch is saying something that I don't hear. All I can think about is that look my mom gave me right before she forgot I existed.

The guys are huddled around me now. I see Jess sitting in the background, trying to keep Rukus still. First, Brock stomps on my chest. Then, Spunk kicks me in the arm and Mitch steps on my sack. After that I quit keeping track of from where the kicks are coming. I just close my eyes, curl up into the fetal position, and take their blows for what seems like an eternity. Eventually, my whole body becomes numb from the cold and the pain. Then, all of a sudden, it stops.

I open my eyes ever so slightly and blood fills my right eye. My vision is cloudy, but I can still make out the image of Jess—the love of my life—standing above me. She appears almost angelic as she looks down on me, with the streetlight shining behind her head like a halo.

The angel spits in my face. Then, she pulls her leg back and kicks me square in the jaw.

I stay lying in the snow as I watch them walk away. The image fades as I close my eyes.

The light shines in my eyes and I wake up for what feels like the last time. A layer of snow about one centimeter thick drapes over my face. I wipe the snow off and look down towards my leg, where Rukus is curled up. I stare at him, expecting the dog to try and kiss me good morning, but aside from his shaking profusely he does not move.

I pull myself up and grab Rukus. I wipe the wet snow off of him and hold him close to my chest. He continues to tremble. He looks up at me with a great amount of effort, and I know I have to get him some help. There is only one place I can go.

I walk to my parents' house. The streets are full of people and I figure it must be about noon the next day. The people all look at me as if they're asking themselves what happened to my face. At my parents' house, I slide my key into the door. I try to shake it into the keyhole, but it doesn't fit. So much for being welcome to stay here, I think.

Luckily, my parents installed a dog door when I got Rukus. I slide him through the flap and knock on the door, hoping that my parents will hear me and take care of him. They will see him shaking and will know what to do. They may be able to take care of him, and if not they'll get him to a vet. The bottom line is that he will be better off with them, than he could ever be with me.

I knock until I see my dad walking down the stairs. Then, I turn around and walk away. My mom is peeking out at me through the curtains. Then, I see my dad's hand grab the curtain and pull it shut.

I keep walking. I don't know where I'm going, nor do I know where I *can* go. All I know is that I need a pick-me-up.

The Little Book of Nothing
M.J. Nicholls

So, Elise sits down every night at six to work on her novel, *Death in the Trees*, but can't concentrate, because across the room her partner, Raymond, shouts abuse at a football match taking place on his laptop. One millionaire hasn't blocked another millionaire, and Raymond knows, with his sixth sense for knowing where the football should be at each precise moment to generate goals, that these men are plonkers, and if he were in charge there wouldn't be such incompetence, and the team would score one million goals in the first two minutes.

Elise can't get past the third sentence because she knows, as sure as she knows that she doesn't love Raymond (or any man, or anything on God's generally quite pointless earth), that her book is a waste of time, and she should give it up, because honestly, what's the point in her writing a book when so many people with talent and brains across the globe are presently engaged in serious, important work, and she—a waitress, an art school dropout—is one of the hopeless masses, keying words onto blank screens in the hope someone might connect to one of her ordered squiggles, her long and winding paragraphs, her long asthmatic paragraphs, with endless commas, commas that lead nowhere, that go on, and on, and on.

Elise is privy to a secret shared by those who spend their lives in rooms, making words appear on pages: writing is the most horrendous thing a person can do, short of attaching electrodes to their nipples, in public, naked, while dogs chew the stumps of their dead frazzled legs, in the rain, in the snow, in the burning flames of hell, in Swindon. She knows, like every other writer, the unpleasant graft of putting words to white, clicking words to oblivion, changing words to other words, to make them better than other writers' words, so that one day, someone sitting on a sofa is stimulated enough to continue looking at your words, to crinkle their lips in a smile of recognition, to laugh at a corny pun, or—at best—to get through a sentence and huff out a "meh", before tossing them aside, forever. This is the dream. To one day have your words sitting on shelves, in discount bins, in warehouses, your words travelling the world, being read by students, Conservatives, the bored, the sad, the lonely, and the insane. To be read, but never heard. To be heard, but never read.

The Dream.

* * *

Raymond, like all devoted and loving partners of writers, thinks Elise is wasting her time and isn't going to earn any serious money sitting before a laptop all night, sweating out sentences, that she should give up *The Dream* and fill her uterus with babies. Elise, like all writers, doesn't listen to her partner, or to anyone who criticises her vocation, knowing that if she did, she couldn't bring herself to put her clothes on in the morning, to throw shirts around her shoulders, and feed her arms through the holes, and do up the buttons. Sitting at that laptop, at six every night, is more important to her than earning money, or eating food, or being in love, or chasing happiness, or taking in oxygen.

It's not something she, or anyone—even those writers she hears saying they love to write, who can squeeze in three thousand words before work, who raise families and smile all the fucking time—can explain. All she knows is that she's a writer, and she wants to kill herself.

*   *   *

Elise leads a life in search of a plot. Her novel is stuffed with them. Catherine, the heroine, spends her time moping around a village, looking at trees and taking ludicrous amounts of methadone. She talks in depth about the trees, because Elise feels that will lend her book more intellectual curiosity. She uses elaborate nature metaphors that evoke the bleak beauty of Thomas Hardy, because Elise thinks all writing must reflect or reference other writing to pitch its tent in the camp of capital-L literature. She does odd things, like licking the trees or taking her pants off and wrapping them around twigs, because Elise doesn't have the guts to write about someone normal. She doesn't hide her depression through forced smiles and stoic mannerisms like Elise does, who can't muster the courage to write about herself, because if she could, she doesn't know what would come out, what solipsistic drivel she would toss onto the page and stare at with her tongue hanging out, paralysed by feeling.

*   *   *

Desmond, the hero, looks out the window and smiles at Catherine draping her pants across twigs, knowing he is to blame for her unhappiness, that he will have dominion over this damaged little girl for so long as he chooses, so long as she keeps taking her methadone, so long as she crawls up to him in bed each night, clinging to his arms in case life should rise up and swallow her. Desmond knows Catherine is afraid of living, is afraid that destiny is cruel, that life will never improve, that she will be stuck here in her big blue pants with Raymond, still on the first page, eating biscuits and drinking coffee as she brings her trembling hands to the keys, in the hope of being less alone, in the hope of filling a silence that can never be answered by the voices buzzing around her, sounds that say everything, but express nothing. As hard as she tries, Desmond becomes Raymond, and the two worlds are inseparable, how she chooses to behave, to be with Raymond, informed by the neurosis of her invented self, closer and closer to the woman who hugs trees and sheds her pants in spontaneous fits.

*   *   *

Elise is going insane. She's almost thirty and has nothing to show for three decades of existence, apart from a clichéd boyfriend and a career that's skirling further along the ice floe into oblivion. If she doesn't get a novel published this year, this month, this week, she will go on a rampage in the town, pulling off the heads of babies and puking down their necks, lobbing grenades at those stucco-fronted homes, where her friends now live with their sprats and their thirty-thousand quid salaries, and their profitable ambitions, peeling the smugness off their faces in strips, until she reigns supreme as The Published Author. If Elise doesn't reach the bestseller list with her miserable book, her miserable worthless book, her *Little Book of Nothing*, she will take four hundred paracetamol, drink a carton of lighter fluid, and fling herself under a train. Elise is not her heroine. She *is* her heroine — really —

but she is not her heroine if anyone asks. Someone like Raymond, who asks: Is she based on you? No, she is not me, she *is* me, but she is definitely *not* me. Shut up.

*   *   *

Elise is disgusted with the human body. Whenever Raymond takes off his clothes and stands before her, she cringes at his sandbags of pectoral sag, and wants to tunnel through the bed to live with the voles, the other bestselling voles, chinking their glasses and accurately quoting Gore Vidal. She used to look upon his legs as two seabed stanchions—support beams to cling to in bed—their legs two pairs of scissors snipping darkness from the world, a perfect cut-out of modern love. Now she can't stand that *thing*—that scallop with salty sacs—can't take it inside of her, because she, too, repulses herself. It's like her skin is slowly being attracted to a magnet in her feet. Her breasts don't jounce. Her legs don't hum. Her vagina looks like Tesco value chicken portions, with extra Ruskoline and tripe. It used to be that she could come so hard she'd see stars. Now, she can orgasm and thread a needle at the same time. If she doesn't do something about her life soon, she'll…have to come up with something to do about her life—soon.

*   *   *

Her prose fails because she wants to be Jeanette Winterson, or Anaïs Nin, or Doris Lessing. She can't make up her mind. So, she uses torturous metaphors about trees. The trees, spindly hanks of madness, upshoots of lunacy as she shrieks, shrieks, shrieks in the park, her knickers around her ankles as she pisses on her legs, lipstick smeared across her cheeks, running towards children, rubbing their heads into her crotch, fucking up against the bark, rubbing her wet cunt against the bark until it bleeds, licking blood off the twigs, fucking kids in the ass. She doesn't know where to stop, because she's half-deranged. She doesn't know where this comes from, this endless slew of arboreal porn and slapstick paedophilia. Sometimes, she goes into the bathroom, paints her lips red, paints her face red, a clown in red-face—the red of menstrual blood, of a woman whose soul is haemorrhaging. She reads her work back and laughs out loud whenever Catherine, *not* her, rapes a child in the ass, sticking it to some little blonde bitch with a pearl-studded dildo, sticking it hard until her cunt splits open—*hahahahahahaha*—then, she goes to vomit in the bathroom.

*   *   *

It is a story of madness, or possibly child abuse, or possibly tree abuse, or about the subjugation of women. Or, about one woman going insane because she has unrealistic expectations, and has grown to hate herself so much that she no longer feels like herself. She is becoming Catherine. She has become vengeance. The day will come when she truly does not care any longer—an exile from herself, a stranger in a strange body.

*   *   *

The day comes when she no longer truly cares. It happens over breakfast, over a bowl of Frosties, a disgusting bowl of Frosties. She tastes the sugar on her tongue and feels sick, sick with sweetness. All she wants to do is tear off her clothes, and eat babies, and fuck trees.

She sits on the sofa all afternoon and dribbles, ignoring the phone, staring at inert pixels on the TV, faking their words, lying to her face—stupid airbrushed liars. She picks up her laptop and the words stream out of her. She writes:

Hello world…this is me, Elise, this is me, not some fake bitch with bigger brains and better prose, this is the real me, here I am, I am here, and I cannot stand myself, I cannot stand to look at myself. My whole world is tied to this useless desire to write, to make people care about this disaffected drivel I put on the page, and I don't even know for what I'm doing it. That's a lie, I do. I want people to read me and understand me, to understand what it feels like to be me, what it feels like to be so alone inside, what it feels like to get so low that you can't bring yourself to eat properly, to make conversation, to live. I know that's a tall order. Why should anyone care about me, about my stupid life? Well, they shouldn't, but that's all we do as writers. We want to draw people nearer in the hope that they understand how awful it feels to be a writer, attempting to write about life, how much more painful it is to write than it is to live. So, this book means nothing. It is my Little Book of Nothing.

*   *   *

She sits and writes this drivel for the whole afternoon. When Raymond comes home, she goes to the library to write in peace. When the library closes, she goes to an all-night café and lets it pour from her, reams of useless self-confession, apologies for herself and her horrible words. Exhausted, she goes home, prints her manuscript, and sighs. She puts it into a padded A4 envelope and writes on the front P.O. BOX NOWHERE. She leaves no return address. She walks to the post box and pushes it through the slot. Back home, she deletes her one copy of the manuscript, clears the recycle bin. She opens a new Word document to confirm what she suspects. Yes, it's over. She will never again write another word. She will never stare at a blank page, wanting to slash her wrists. She will never again be tethered to the page, never again feel the life draining from her. She feels free, free to again live and love, free to live a clichéd life.

*   *   *

Once again, her life begins. She wakes at a clichéd eight

o'clock and eats a clichéd bowl of cereal, and has a clichéd talk with Raymond, her clichéd boyfriend. She conducts the ordinary day with the most extraordinary passion she can, serving coffees and teas with the biggest, widest smile her face can contain, laughing hysterically at each banal observation made by Dim Jenny. In the evening, she prepares the most flavoursome and delicious boil-in-the-bag dinner for two, and savours each spoonful, licking her fork clean as though the slurry gravy were golden caviar from God's bistro. She makes passionate love to Raymond, beautiful and perfect Raymond, the beautiful and perfect man, with his delicious body, rolling her tongue around his humming folds, driving her to fits of ecstasy, harder and harder, until she passes out from ordinary happiness. She will never again write another word. She is the happiest woman alive.

Clinic of Lost Monsters
Cornelius Fortune

All of her nightmares began the same—with someone holding her hand…then, letting go…

…the ground rushing towards her and blank faces that watched her come to pieces in black, and white, and red in *extreme* close-up. They were all there: her neighbors, and her roommate, and her daughter Clara.

"Don't let go," said Clara. "You mustn't let go, or the game loses meaning."

"Clara?" Yet, it wasn't Clara. It was what she'd imagined Clara to become some thirteen years into an improbable future.

She awoke, cold and nauseous, her gown meshed to her skin, and the werewolf snoring in the corner of the room. She closed the window.

It was always anxiety. Tomorrow, she was going to be back in the living world again. How would she adjust — saying goodbye to old friends and drinking tea that hadn't come from a dim-lit dispenser?

*   *   *

"How do you feel, Martha?"

"Quite shaken, if you really want to know the truth. I've waited for this day. Now I'm afraid of it."

They were in Dr. Greenway's office with the picture of the marble fawn, atop a rusted truck abandoned to the elements, in a vaguely New Yorkish setting. It hung over her desk in view, so that the patient could look at it if they chose not to stare into Dr. Greenway's petulant eyes. The clock on the wall glowed the same green as that of the light above Dr. Greenway's desk, which smelled faintly of nail polish remover.

Dr. Greenway—she noted for the first time—was very pretty in an Agnes Moorehead kind of way, though she didn't strike her as the type to bear children.

"What are you afraid of?" asked Dr. Greenway. "It seems to me that you've adjusted well, considering the trauma you've endured."

She looked up from writing. "Do you have dreams of *Clara* anymore?"

"No," Martha lied.

"You do not believe that she's still alive…that she haunts you?"

"Not at all," said Martha, rubbing her kneecaps and trying not to appear too nervous. She picked at the tiny hole in her stockings like it was a scab. "*It* died on March 3, 1999, in a clinic for family planning. I killed it because he wanted it dead."

"He?"

"My fiancé, Billy Norton," she said. "We met in Manhattan at a poetry reading. It wasn't love, not at first—that came afterwards—but you see…it was like the end of the world to him, like I had sentenced him to death. I had to do something to keep his love."

"Because he was much younger, less experienced?"

"Of legal age," she assured Dr. Greenway. "Nineteen. But it wasn't about the baby. I was thirty-one. Five months later he proposed to me, and I said yes without thinking. He proposed to me out of pity—"

A small beep issued from the phone on Dr. Greenway's desk. "Excuse me," she said, and picked up the phone.

"Oh...hi Dr. Modlin. Yes, everything seems to be in order. I'm here with her now..." Her face changed. She looked at her watch. "I had completely forgotten. Is that at six PM? Okay, thanks. Yes—I'll be sure to tell her. Goodbye now."

She hung up the phone.

"Am I free to go?"

"Of course," said Dr. Greenway, "I see no reason to detain you further. Dr. Modlin sends his best—he's in New England lecturing."

She stood up and walked to the door. Martha followed, slinging her purse over her arm, feeling the cold draft slipping through the tear in her stocking. "Take care of yourself, Clara. If there are any problems—"

"*Martha*, Dr. Greenway, you called me *Clara*."

"Did I," she asked, "How strange? I thought I said Martha."

Dr. Greenway shook her head. "It doesn't really matter now, does it Martha? You're cured."

"Yes," said Martha, "*cured*."

"Goodbye Martha."

"Goodbye Dr. Greenway," said Martha. "I feel much better now. I'm not afraid of going."

"Nor should you be."

"Would it be okay if I said goodbye to the others?"

"I don't think that would be a good idea at all. Goodbye Martha."

They shook hands and Martha went out.

*   *   *

She had acquired little over the eight months of making her home here. Her life was compact enough to fit inside a handbag and a small suitcase, of which she'd won at a state fair raffle.

"Mom," said Clara, walking beside Martha.

She ignored Clara, walking down the hallway and whistling.

"Mom? C'mon, don't go freaky-weird on me now."

Martha stopped at the elevator and waited.

A young orderly passed by and Clara smiled at his departing buttocks. "Oh he's cute," said Clara, smacking her lips. "Did you see his eyes? Did you see how green they were? Mom, you can stop acting now."

The elevator doors opened. Three doctors filed out. Martha stepped in and the doors closed. "You know why I'm upset, don't you?" asked Martha.

"Why, Mom?"

"Try harder."

"I was just having a little fun with her." Clara stuck out her lip. "Don't be mad with me."

"I'm not mad, Clara," said Martha, "but I expect a little more from you." She pressed the 11 button.

"Are we going to see Mr. Bachelon and Mr. Soukoup?"

"Yes," said Martha, "against doctor's orders. They've all become…friends. I can't leave without saying goodbye."

The doors opened and Clara floated behind her. She didn't say a word, which possibly meant that her feelings were hurt. There'd be time to make up later.

Five elderly men and an elderly woman sat in the lounge, gathered around the television: a werewolf, a vampire, a mummy, Frankenstein's monster, and Frankenstein's bride. They were monsters, and their families had locked them away for their strange beliefs.

Mr. Bachelon turned. His mouth had the collapsed look of missing dentures—he hadn't bothered to put them in. "We were beginning to think you weren't going to say goodbye, Marty."

"You know better than that," said Martha.

"I'm sure Dr. Greenway discouraged you from seeing us," Mr. Soukoup, the mummy, said. His wrists were lined with cuts, scabbed over a dozen times—raw, black.

"She figures, since she's gotten the crazy out of you, you shouldn't be conversing with the likes of us," said Frankenstein's bride. "We're a bad influence, you know, a clinic of lost monsters. That's what wolf-breath calls us."

The werewolf snorted. His name was Dr. Jonathon Eugene and he rarely said anything at all. His eyes lit up. "Clara, my dear…how are you? Come sit by Uncle John, I've a question to ask you."

Clara sat beside him.

The six of them talked about the world, and of time and perception, and of why they were so different from the rest of society, while the werewolf and Clara watched a game show on television.

Mr. Bachelon shook his head. "You're still having those dreams, aren't you?"

"Yes," said Martha. "Why? What do you think they mean?"

"Dreams are, of themselves, never a good thing with creatures like us. Consider it an omen—a warning from beyond this world, perhaps, even the future. These things are so elusive. My opinion is that you and Clara should take the first train as far as it will go. The murders are starting again and your existences could be in danger. That, I have no doubt."

"Don't let him scare you," said Frankenstein's bride. "He's a cynic and believes in every conspiracy ever formulated."

"John F. Kennedy and Elvis are still alive," said Frankenstein's monster. "I had breakfast with them at a restaurant in Detroit."

"I think you're confusing reality with a movie," his wife said.

"Yes, all of you are." Dr. Greenway studied them with her arms folded and her teeth barred. "Visiting hours are over Martha."

"But I—"

"I've taken the liberty of calling a cab for you—the expenses have been pre-paid. Now say goodbye to your friends. It's time for them to take their medicine."

Martha kissed each of them while Dr. Greenway looked on, irritably.

"Take care of your selves," Martha said to her friends, the ones who understood what it was like to be a monster among men. "Dr. Greenway—"

"That will be all Martha."

"Okay, okay…" said Martha, "I'm leaving."

Martha turned and began walking to the elevators, when she heard a loud snap ring across the hall. Then, a round of stifled laughter came from the monsters. Dr. Greenway was rubbing her back, with a puzzled look on her face.

In the elevator Martha said, "Clara, you know what I'm going to say. Why is it that you try to make life so difficult for your mother?"

"Oh, Mom, don't be so dramatic…she had it coming. Her bra was too tight, so I adjusted it for her."

Despite Martha's resolve to remain straight-faced, she broke into laughter, which caused Clara to break into laughter. For the first time in months they felt comfortable with one another, and could laugh—together—in the shared confines of a musty elevator.

*   *   *

The house was as she remembered it, minus maybe the dust and the coldness of the floor.

She never remembered it being so cold before, maybe because Billy was no longer here. Either way, she didn't like it. The whole thing crumbled and it was all because of Clara — no, it was not Clara's fault. Clara wanted to live. She had every right to come back and haunt her, remind her of all that could have been. She regretted her decision and, over time, began hating Billy for it.

"Mom?" said Clara. "You're crying."

They were at the dinner table. Martha had made too much roast and carrot stew, momentarily forgetting that Clara did not eat—at least, not food.

She hadn't noticed the tears either. Martha reflexively touched her face, and her fingers came away wet.

"Memories, is all Clara. I'm fine really. I don't know if I want to live in this house, anymore."

"Then why not move?" asked Clara enthusiastically. "We could live in Paris or Nice, or Germany…"

"I don't know if I want to move that far away," said Martha, wiping her mouth, "but a change would be good."

The phone rang. Martha picked it up and a look passed over her face. She didn't say anything, but hung the phone up and sat back down at the table.

"Mom?"

"Yes?"

"What's going on?" Clara asked. "Who was on the other end of the phone?"

Martha gathered the corners of the tablecloth in her clenched fists. "It was your father. He wants to see you."

…the dream started in her bedroom, as she watched herself from high on the ceiling, clinging to it like a spider with Clara's hand in hers.

They floated out of the window and into the sky, the wind cold and blowing through their nightgowns. Martha didn't feel at all scared. The dream always went this way…down they descended—upon a glade—touched by dying city lights and foliage overgrown and outstretched, which covered the old truck. From atop the truck, a marble fawn blinked its inky eyes and then scurried off.

"This is how I remember it happening," said Martha.

They swooped in low, hand in hand, landing softly in a brush of wildflowers. Behind them lay a torn New York, somewhere in the future—this park, somewhere in the past, stilled time, deep impressions where feet have trod across the high grass.

Near a fountain that spurted clear crystal, Martha saw a younger version of herself atop the marble fawn, riding it close. She stroked its ears affectionately and dismounted. The fawn stood upright, his legs, and arms, and face becoming that of a man, but his eyes still holding the dark inky confluence. They kissed, and played, and tumbled in the grass.

"Was I ever that young?" asked Martha.

"Mom, you were only thirty-one."

"That seems so long ago."

Startled from their light passion, the two looked at the mother and daughter. The man—the marble fawn—who was her father, stood up. "My dear, Clara…give your father a hug."

He spread his arms.

The younger Martha didn't bother to cover up. Her blouse blew in the breeze, her rosy nipples hardened by the cool wind. "This is what you've always wanted. The monster wasn't

Clara. It was always, irrevocably, you. How could you kill our unborn child?"

"*You wanted it. I did it because you said it would make you happy—that we would be happy together," Martha said, feeling Clara's hand slipping away.*

She was seeking refuge in the arms of a father she did not know, tearing herself from the monster who'd murdered her.

"*No, Clara, don't! Don't leave me!" It all became slow. Mud, and flowers, and leaves held her legs in place. She stumbled and fell...*

...the glass shards rushing about her.

Martha opened her eyes.

"Clara? Clara?" she said. "Oh, my God, Clara! Clara don't leave me." She pressed her face in the pillow and filled it with tears.

The werewolf said, "Martha, Martha. You're dreaming. Wake up Martha."

Though, she didn't want to talk about it, and reluctantly fell back to sleep.

*   *   *

"How do you feel Martha?"

"I still have nightmares."

"They will pass," said Dr. Greenway. "Your husband is here to pick you up."

"My...husband?"

"Why yes, don't you remember?"

The door opened and in stepped Billy, wearing a suit that was too small, and a blue and green tie that was far too long. "Oh, I'm sorry."

"No, that's quite all right Mr. Norton," said Dr. Greenway. "We were just finishing up."

"Is everything...okay?" he asked, joining Martha's side. He squeezed her hand reassuringly.

"She has occasional nightmares—that's to be expected."

"Then, she's not cured?"

"She's on the road to recovery, and what follows will be entirely up to her," Dr. Greenway answered.

Martha couldn't tell if she was still dreaming, or if she had finally wakened. It didn't matter—Billy was going to take care of her. She glanced at the painting on Dr. Greenway's wall. The painting was different. It depicted a prism with shattered glass, and bold colors shooting throughout. She wondered where the marble fawn had gone.

"When did you change the painting on the wall?" Martha asked.

Dr. Greenway stared at Martha and tried a smile that didn't come off quite right. "This painting has been hanging here for the past three years…that's the effect it's supposed to have. The artist I purchased it from said that it reveals 'angles on life'. I don't entirely agree with him, but others have remarked upon differences in the painting with each viewing."

Dr. Greenway pushed away from her desk and stood up. "To tell the truth, I thought it blended in well with the furniture, and that it would be something nice for my patients to look at besides me, or the wall."

She opened the door. "I have an appointment to keep—in another part of the facility."

Billy helped Martha to her feet and they met Dr. Greenway at the door. "I'd like to thank you for all your help," he said.

"It's what I'm here for," Dr. Greenway said. "There are some forms you need to sign before leaving. As for you, Mrs. Norton, I expect to hear good things from you, and please contact me if anything's wrong."

"I will," said Martha.

"Take care of your selves," the doctor replied.

They shook hands and Billy and Martha walked the length of the hallway in silence. Martha purchased one last cup of tea.

*   *   *

At home, Billy made Martha as comfortable as possible.

He cooked for her, massaged her feet. They took long walks together and he even spoke of wanting to start a family. She wanted so to mention Clara's name, because she missed her, missed being haunted by her. Perhaps, the therapy had worked.

She thought of the others whose families had left them there—that clinic of lost monsters. Each one of them shattered lives, touched by the cruelties of war, abuse, neglect: a vampire, a werewolf, Frankenstein's monster, a mummy, and Frankenstein's bride. They truly existed and didn't need anyone's acknowledgement, or approval, for them to hold on to their convictions. Each of them practiced magic of a sort—a dark magic that twisted reality and dream—so, he allowed it all to happen without pause or regret. Maybe Dr. Greenway had in fact cured her. That wouldn't be so bad…would it?

In the basement, she searched for the dead rats and puppies she'd given Clara (who liked the taste of their souls, their life force). There was no trace of the past five years. The destruction of their marriage seemed—itself— a dream.

"I want you to know," said Billy, "that I forgive you. I don't blame you for what happened. I don't expect you to say anything. You did it all for me, and you've been the same. I'm to blame for this. If you still want to divorce me, that's entirely up to you."

They were sitting in bed with the television on. "But if you want to really start over, we can do it. You can move forward again, because there is no Clara to stand in our way. Don't you see it?"

Yet, she couldn't see it. She saw the dark inky flood of his eyes and the pricking up of his ears. His muzzle mouthed the words: "Let's try it again. I promise it will be better, that I will make it up to you."

It touched her, breathed heavily, and put itself inside her. She let it tire itself, and soon the marble fawn (Billy, her Billy, dear sweet Billy—how she loved him…how she wanted it all to be different) slept.

The curtains blew inward and she lay still, cold and empty. Dr. Greenway had taken Clara from her. What would she do? How could she live? What sort of life would she and Billy have together?

He built the home from his own design.

They were supposed to be happy, but he didn't want her. He wanted what her body would produce for him, now that her illness was *controlled*. He again wanted to control her, as before.

"Clara," whispered Martha. "Clara, please come back. Come back to me."

Staring down at her were the monsters she knew so well. They talked together, talked of their families, of their illnesses and the subjective state of the mind's theater.

"Martha, come with us," they said. "We're leaving the clinic and want you to join us. We're going to live forever, projected on screens of silver, held in the imaginations of many. We will not be forgotten. They will make moving pictures of us. We will become the subject of metaphor. Come with us," they said.

Martha rose from the bed. "But where's Clara?"

They pointed outside.

Martha opened the terrace doors and saw Clara floating outside. "It's time, Mom."

Dr. Greenway smiled at Martha. "The umbilical cord was never severed. You see…it stays connected to the world of spirit."

She felt a bulge in her nightgown, and the thick umbilical leading from her to Clara.

Dr. Greenway held her hand. "It's okay, Martha, you've been waiting to do this."

Her hand was warm, and strong, and reassuring to her. Dr. Greenway let go and Martha slipped over the side of the railing. She hung there, gasping.

Five flights below, in freeze-frame, was the ground.

"Please," she said.

The monsters stared down at her and said nothing.

She felt the cord loosening.

"Don't let go," said Clara. "You mustn't let go, or the game loses meaning…"

She hung there as long as she could possibly stand it.

Her hand slipped and she went down, down, downward.

Clara whispered in her ear, "Mom, don't let go…it's almost over. Don't cut the umbilical…"

She saw the faces of the monsters and the ground embraced her—shattered into a thousand pieces, black, and white, and red.

*   *   *

She felt something being pulled away from her eyes, and she screamed.

"Martha—it's okay," said the voice of the doctor. "You're in a clinic on Fifth Boulevard. It is the year Twenty-Forty-Seven. You came to our office three weeks ago to…consider your options. We offered the holographic program—dubbed, *Lost Monsters*. Do you remember any of this?"

She was slowly coming out of it. "You signed up for our trial period. Your insurance is covering eighty-five percent of the charge. Would you like us to bill the rest to your personal account?"

"I don't know," she said.

"We'll take that as a yes."

Robots worked tirelessly in the white room, handing her holo-tapes on the way out. "We hope the experience of jacking into the mind of your unborn child was a fruitful one, and has given you something to think out. Thank you for trying our simulation at Rudgers Family Dimensions. Goodbye."

Out on the street, the harsh mist of noontide caught her by surprise. She touched her stomach and remembered that it was still inside her—the thing that her and Billy had made. What was it called in the simulation?

"Clara?" she called softly. "Clara, can you hear me?" When the voice didn't come, she raised her collar and walked home.

Beneath her feet she could feel the steady cracking of broken glass and the electric faces with dark, black eyes, following her down the neo-emblazoned street.

The Head
James Beaton

Thomas found a most peculiar love.

He wasn't the sort to fall in love easily, so he had to allow for it when it happened.

I met him when I was out for an evening stroll on a blustery winter night. He was alone in Riverdale Park when I first saw him, an aimless shadow floating against the white background.

"Stormy night," he bellowed through the wind as he drew near. The forceful wind almost stole his words from my ear.

"Indeed," I responded.

"Out for a walk?" he asked, an obvious conversational question.

"Yes, even though it's a good night for being in. If I didn't like storms so much, I might be in front of a warm fire."

"I hear you. There's something lovely and quiet about it, even though it's so wild. You have to respect it. I met my love on a night like this. I saved her from the storm."

"She must have been grateful."

"I would say."

He noticed my shivering and recalled a time when if someone met a stranger in the cold, they would be kind enough to invite them in for tea and warmth.

"Hospitality has been lost in the big cities. Would you like to have some tea?" he asked. "I don't live far from here."

My fingers were numb and I desperately craved warmth.

"Why, that would be lovely," I said, both with gratitude and slight hesitation.

Strangers rarely invite each other into their homes. Yet, I am a man of some size and strength, so I could protect myself.

"I'm Thomas," he said. "I would shake but I am reluctant to remove my hands from my gloves with this wind."

"I understand," I replied, "Liam."

"A pleasure."

His house was a fifteen minute walk from the park. The granite stone exterior protruded through the tops of the tall pines surrounding it. The palatial quarters emanated immediate warmth with lights glowing orange through the first floor windows. With a house like this, I figured he was either a man of some means, or he was fortunate enough to have an inheritance.

We ascended the concrete steps and he fumbled with his keys, which I suspected was from his own frigid fingers. We entered the porch and the welcoming heat eliminated any hesitation I may have held for spending time with this nostalgic stranger. After I removed my boots and coat, Thomas signaled for me to enter the living room.

"I'm going to make some tea. I apologize for leaving you alone, but I won't be ten minutes. Please look around and make yourself at home."

The living room felt like an old library. On one side of the room there were stacks of books, neatly placed on mahogany bookshelves. On the other side, there were shelves filled with ornaments and oddities. The lighting made everything golden yellow, as illuminated by small candles. There was a deep, red area rug in the center of the floor that protected the well-polished wood below it.

I initially settled into an antique, dark red leather chair—with arms that matched the bookshelves—but was inspired to look around. Being observant can offer enough of a window into a person's interests to avoid awkward silences and conversation lags. Often people will talk about whatever oddities they collect. It allows them to tell you about something which has meaning to them. Sometimes, the stories suggest more about the people than they do the items.

On the opposite side of the room, sitting on the shelf, was a ship in a bottle (a barquentine, one of the old cargo sailing ships of the nineteenth century). He seemed lonely, so I imagined that was how he kept his mind occupied in the evenings. He probably focused in on that arduous detail oriented task.

Then, I saw it.

Over on the table against the wall, near the window, sat a strange ornament. Unlike the other items, this one stood out as lacking a classic or antique appearance. No…it couldn't be, I thought, it can't be real.

It was! It was a dried human head.

It did not smell—and looked several years old—but it appeared to have some makeup and powder on it, which suggested to me Thomas was attempting to make it look…less dead. My inclination was to pick up and further inspect it, but I did not dare. Whatever this was, I would have to leave it for Thomas to tell me.

I couldn't help but wonder if the head was some sort of *trophy* from a murder he'd committed. He was a loner, eccentric, and assertive enough to invite strangers to visit his place. On the other hand, he was hospitable, had a gentle and calming quality about him, and was charming. I wasn't an expert in profiling murderers, but he just didn't seem the type.

Thomas returned to the room while I was standing next to the head. I only knew he was there when he placed the tea on the coffee table and the cup clinked against the saucer. I turned with a start, and must have been wearing a guilty look upon my face.

He offered the tea to me, spilling it over the edge of the cup.

"Darn," he exclaimed, "so messy. I can make you a new cup if you'd like."

"No, that's okay. It's perfectly fine," I said, noting to myself how something as trivial as a little spilled tea upset him. Possibly obsessive, overly orderly...I thought.

He lowered himself onto the couch with a rather serious look on his face, took his tea in his hand and sipped. It must have been too hot, as he flinched and returned it to the table, spilling more.

"I see you were looking at my specimen," he said, his eyes shifting enough to betray his calm demeanor.

"Yes, you collect some interesting items," I said. "The head appears realistic."

"I try to put it away, for obvious reasons, if I have guests. I wasn't expecting company. In fact, I hardly ever have anybody over. I apologize. That shouldn't be left out for anybody to see." He anxiously walked across the room. "I can put it away. You probably find it disturbing."

"It's fine there. Is it real?" I asked.

He stopped when I queried this. His shoulders slumped with what I could only interpret as resignation.

"Yes," he replied. "Yes, it is real. You are the first who has ever seen it, other than me. I have always been very careful about people knowing I have it. Twenty years now without any discovery." He said this with the tone of someone confessing a terrible crime.

"How did you get it?" I asked, pushing things further.

"Just one moment, please. I have to clean up the tea from the table," he said, leaving abruptly.

I wasn't sure what I should do. Part of me wanted to exit quickly. He could have been getting an axe. He could have been planning to decapitate me, to make it a set. Yet, another part of me wanted to stay, so I could hear the story of how he acquired it. My intuition told me he wasn't the murdering type.

He returned with a kitchen towel and meticulously cleaned the liquid off the table. "The hot liquid can stain the wood. It's best to wipe it away as soon as possible." He paused, disappointed. "I think it may have stained."

He returned to his seat and carefully picked up his tea from the table, this time being careful not to spill any. He regained his composure and inhaled a deep breath, as if he was going to be underwater for a while.

"Now where were we? It's not a story I have ever told. Yet, I fear that by not saying anything, and leaving you to wonder, you will think I am involved in sordid activities. I can assure you that it is not the case. Perhaps, my only shortcoming is poor judgment—that and loneliness. I haven't hurt anyone. It was all coincidence. If I can ask a favor—insofar a stranger, who has a human head on a table can ask for one—could you not repeat the story?"

"I assure you that your story is safe."

It really was, for I had no inclination to reveal to anybody the activities of this man, nefarious or otherwise.

"This is very good of you. I must admit it's nice to find someone who I can tell. Most people would rush to judgment upon hearing something like this. You still might. However, if I die, at least one person will know the story, a story that friends and family would not understand. There will be someone who will know that I did not kill anybody."

So, he began with what I can only describe as a well-rehearsed, but never spoken, monologue.

*   *   *

It was a night much like tonight, when I was out for a walk. I saw something protruding from the snow, close to where you were standing when we began talking. Imagine my surprise when I saw it was a freshly severed head. Its eyes had been removed, and scars ran across the pale frozen face. There was no sign of anybody else, although it was snowing heavily, so it was likely that any tracks would have been covered quickly. There was some blood around the head in the snow, so I thought it might be somewhat fresh.

I couldn't believe my discovery. I had never seen a dead body before, and there was this head, just sitting in the snow. Most people would be horrified. They would have backed away from the head and called the police, so that this heinous crime could be solved. I, however, did not. In fact, my mind went in a different, less conventional direction.

It was all so exciting. I couldn't believe my luck. Nothing like that ever happened to me.

I kneeled in the snow next to it. What could have led to this, I thought.

I developed theories, all of which seemed unlikely. Perhaps, someone else found it elsewhere and then brought it there. Perhaps, there was a murder and the killer had to leave in a hurry, and disposed of it in the park. Perhaps, someone else found it and took it here, where it would be found.

My fingers stroked through its frozen hair in fascination. The head stared toward the sky, while white flecks of snow fell into its black encrusted holes, from where its eyes once looked upon the world. Its mouth was agape, as if it was about to say something.

This was the closest I had been to someone in a while.

Perhaps, it was fascination. Perhaps, it was loneliness. I decided to take it home. If the police knew of the head, they would be most interested. They would probably send a team of investigators to search the area for a day or two. What would they have found? Nothing. The snow covered everything. If the rest of the body was somewhere, and presumably it was, that would be more than enough to alert the authorities that something was wrong. There was no body that I could see. I know what you might say: "What if that was the only evidence of the crime?" I have no response to that. In retrospect, I likely hindered an investigation. I was prepared to listen to the radio, watch the television, and read the newspaper to ensure that if there were missing people, then I could return the head to where I found it.

Despite the unbearable cold and wind, I removed my coat to wrap it around my find. This wasn't for protection, but rather to keep it from the view of any people walking by, who might think it strange or inappropriate that I was walking down the street with a head. If someone saw me holding this head, and jauntily walking along the sidewalk, they would make assumptions that would lead to nothing but trouble for me. They might have mistakenly assumed I was the killer. Thankfully, I did not have far to go, and was able to return home without running into anybody.

I needed to warm myself and think more about what I should do. I made some tea and turned on the radio to listen to the news, just in case there were any reports of headless bodies being found. Then, I returned to the living room and unveiled the head from my coat.

Guilt enveloped me.

I knew I should have reported it. I started thinking, or perhaps rationalizing, that it was too late to change the course of my actions. Police might suspect me as being involved, and if not involved in the murder, having obstructed justice. I could return it, but if any of my hair was on it, or anybody saw me in the area, I would be considered a suspect. I didn't want to go to jail for something that I hadn't done. Even if I was found not-guilty, there would probably be a negative reaction to my taking it from the park, which would tarnish my reputation. I was so torn.

I drank my tea and whispered to the head that everything would be okay. This is where you might think I am strange—if you do not already possess such cogitations. However, everything I say is true.

I was certain the head thanked me. It spoke. Not the way you speak. It didn't move its dead, frozen lips. However, I heard it. It told me that it was grateful and hoped to stay a while, because it had been through so much. It just needed some stability. Most people would be terrified if this was happening to them. Initially, I was stupefied, wondering if I might be going crazy.

I placed my hand on its still-frozen cheek and told it everything would be okay and that I would take care of it.

I left it on the coffee table when I retired for the night. Despite the cold wind causing my windows to rattle, I slept well that night. When I rested my head on the pillow and closed my eyes, I saw the head floating on the insides of my eyelids. It was smiling and emanating warmth.

I could barely contain my excitement to see it again when I awoke. In the morning I ran downstairs with the exuberance of a young child at Christmas, only to discover it was leaking a reddish fluid all over the table. I retrieved a roasting pan from the kitchen and placed the head inside, so that it wouldn't stain the coffee table or the floor.

Then, it asked me: "Why do I have to be in this pan? It makes me feel as if you are going to bake me."

It stared at me with its hollowed eyes. Its mouth gaped open, with its lips parted enough for me to see its teeth. At one time it probably had a beautiful smile. In the light it appeared as if its nose was fractured. While normally I wouldn't think these things to be attractive, I found them strangely endearing.

"I wouldn't bake you. How cruel would that be? I quite like you," I responded in my attempt to ensure it did not panic from its placement in the baking pan.

I carried the head into the kitchen, so I could sit with it while I ate breakfast. I could sense its anxiety and its worry that I might have something terrible planned. Obviously, it had reason to be skeptical of human motivations. Someone had already separated it from its body, which is arguably one of the most extreme acts imaginable. It was one of those experiences that would make trusting in the future difficult.

I made my breakfast: home fries, eggs, and bacon (which are always a favorite of mine). I like to season the potatoes with oregano and parsley, and add a little diced onion in for flavor.

The head was in front of me while I ate. We didn't talk, but talking wasn't necessary. I simply enjoyed its presence. I turned on the news and there was nothing about a decapitated body being found or anybody going missing. This offered me some relief. I was growing more certain that even if I did hear of a body being found, I couldn't alert the authorities of my find. As well, the head seemed happy here, and despite being dead, the company was welcomed.

I was late for work because I spent my early morning drinking tea and stroking the head's face. I was convinced it moaned as I ran my fingers over its pallid face.

For as long as possible I stayed home, but eventually had to leave because people would notice if I didn't come to work. As a senior manager I have a certain amount of leeway, but if people start asking where I was, and I didn't show, then it would not look good. As I was preparing to leave for work, I could sense the head was unhappy. Such thoughts were nonsense. It was just a head! It had no thoughts or feelings — it wasn't possible for it to miss me. Nevertheless, I believed there was sadness in its expression. Its gouged eyes and bluish lips revealed disappointment.

The day was like most others with the exception that I was completely unfocused on the work I should have been doing. I was supposed to be preparing for a meeting, and as I sat at my office desk, I thought about the head at home thawing in the roasting pan. It was so frustrating that I couldn't tell anybody about my discovery. They would most certainly disapprove. If I told anybody, it would all be over. They would make me report it, and would probably think me strange, and perhaps even dangerous.

The day crawled like a sedated snail. The hands on the clock barely moved. The meeting was painful. I had to make a presentation about the tasks on which I had been working for the past month. Halfway through the presentation, I envisioned the head sitting in front of me, watching curiously as I spoke. I couldn't continue. I stopped talking and one of the other senior managers asked if I was okay. I told him I was fine.

Throughout the afternoon people were coming into my office, asking me questions about different projects. I couldn't focus enough to adequately respond, so I left many of my coworkers befuddled. How I wished that I could have brought the head with me into my office.

The day finally ended. Someone asked me to work on something as I was leaving, and I told them I couldn't because I had an important commitment. Normally I would stay if people asked, as I had nothing beyond work. My coworker laughed and asked if it was a romantic interest, suggesting that perhaps a new love interest was responsible for my sudden absentmindedness. I smiled and left.

I didn't go to the pub, as I normally did after work. Usually, I would go and have a stout, while watching whatever was on television. Instead, I was excited to get home.

As soon as I walked into the house, the pungent smell worked its way into my nose. The roasting tray was filled with unsavory juices. I touched the forehead and it was no longer cold. I carried the head to the bathroom, so I could flush the liquid. I gagged as the sour fumes entered my throat.

I emptied the pan into the toilet, flushing away the rancid fluids and almost dropping the head into the bowl. I decided to clean it, to try and make it smell a bit better. I lathered it with shampoo and washed it using cold water. I wasn't sure what hot water would do to the decomposition process. Its hair did look better than before.

I returned it to the pan. I was happy that it smelled fresher, but couldn't help being displeased with the underlying smell of rot. That evening I felt completely comfortable with everything. I picked up a book and read. I wasn't even conscious of it, but I was reading aloud. It was enjoyable to read to something. That evening I gave it a name. I called it Head.

The next month was difficult because Head was decaying and smelling quite bad, which made spending time together challenging. I couldn't touch it like before, as its skin was becoming fragile and its hair was falling out. Admittedly, the visual of decaying flesh was less appealing than in the beginning.

I would come home and be faced with an overwhelming stench so strong, that I could barely be in the same room. Head would greet me with excitement, eager to spend time together. I thought about putting

Head into the refrigerator, but there was no way I could ever do that. How would I see it, then? If I wanted to have it around, then it would have to go through this process. The first few months of any relationship can sometimes be the most difficult. Worthwhile things always involve some sacrifice.

There were a few occasions where I was almost caught with Head. Once, I went to work and was wearing a shirt that had the lingering smell of Head. Several people commented on how terrible I smelled, and one person asked if I was dying. I laughed and changed the topic immediately.

The closest I was to ever getting caught was when my aunt visited me, unexpectedly, from out of town. I was reading in the dining room, with Head, when I heard a knock at the door. I ignored it and pretended I wasn't home. The knocking continued, this time harder. I became worried that someone called the police. I took Head from the room and placed it in the oven (without turning it on, of course). Head didn't want to be hidden in the oven, but I reassured it that it couldn't be discovered, and it was the only way we could be together.

When I opened front door, I discovered my sixty-three year old aunt, Lillian. She barreled past me without saying hello, and within minutes was complaining about the putrid smell. Lillian was always the one to lose her filter, and say the most outrageous things at family gatherings.

"What is that horrible smell? Don't you ever clean? It smells like something died. Let me take out your garbage. Is there a dead raccoon in your kitchen? This wouldn't happen if you had a woman in your life. What's wrong with you, anyway? No woman is good enough for you?"

I told her everything was fine and that it was a sewage problem. She expressed skepticism at my excuse for the smell, indicating that she'd smelled sewage before and this wasn't sewage. I offered her tea, hoping that would distract her, but she was insistent on wanting to help. It took a good twenty minutes to get her into the living room, sitting down. I did not want her snooping around the kitchen.

Lillian gossiped about the family, mentioning the smell every ten minutes or so. She told me the same old stories about my cousin's failing marriage, my uncle's lack of motivation, my brother in-law's tumor, and my grandmother's diabetes. I'd heard all those stories many times before.

Eventually—with a gesture she would not miss—I looked at my watch and told her I had work to catch up on, as well as some pressing matters with which to deal. At first, she refused. She claimed that she didn't have anywhere to stay, and if she spent the week with me that she could clean whatever was causing that God-awful smell. Apparently, she'd travelled to the city without arranging for any accommodation. I felt guilty saying no, but there was no way I could allow her to discover Head.

I thanked her politely, indicating that my work demanded solitude. I offered her money for a hotel, and told her that I would let her know if I needed help. On her way out she expressed concern for me, and suggested that she might come for a more extended visit, to make sure everything was okay.

After I was certain she was gone, I removed Head from the oven. It was angry with me for placing it in the oven, forcing me to explain why it would have been very bad if Lillian discovered it. I realized that if the authorities ever did come here asking questions, they would be very aware of the smell and possibly suspicious enough to conduct a search. As difficult as it was going to be, we had to be apart during the decomposition period. It was the only way we could safely be together forever.

My plan was this: There was a hot water radiator in the attic. It would mean a separation period, but by following this, we could be together with much less risk. I would put Head there with the hope that a low level of heat, over a couple of months, would slowly dry it out. I would also enclose it in a container, so as not to attract flies. Insects were quite a concern for me. I could imagine how seeing Head with maggots on its face would alter my perception.

Head ended up being there for six months. Those were difficult days, and despite it being just upstairs, I opted to not see it. The day I carried it to the attic, it accused me of not caring, suggesting that I was punishing it. Each night I could hear crying. Endless sobs flooded down the stairs. Imagine hearing someone you love crying every night, but being unable to do anything about it. If I went upstairs, I knew it would plead for me to take it down. I suppose I could have stayed in the attic, as well, but I am accustomed to a certain level of cleanliness and order.

I never thought I was lonely before Head, but after it came into my life, our distance revealed an emptiness I didn't know was there. To occupy myself during the drying period, I drew pictures of it frozen in the snow, as I found it that day. I stopped paying close attention to the news. No body was found, nor was anybody missing. This meant nobody was looking for it.

After the six months, the skin was dry enough for me to bring it downstairs. Admittedly, seeing the dried skin pulled back over its skull and straw-like hair made me think of it as more odd than beautiful.

I made a cake and prepared a nice dinner. We ate our first meal together, each of us with so much about which to talk. Sounds odd, doesn't it? Yet, everything was delicious, and that night marked the beginning of a beautiful future for us.

I always made sure that on the rare occasion of company, I placed Head out of view from visitors. I suppose with time, and no visitors, I became careless. I never thought about it when I invited you over. Before I leave the house, I should always put it away. You never know what can happen.

That is why Head sits there today.

*   *   *

Thomas had already placed his tea back on the table without me noticing.

"I do hope you leave this between us," he said. "I know this may be a great burden on you, but I have one thing to ask."

"What is that?"

"If somehow you hear of my death, and also hear of me being called a murderer, can you tell the police what I've told you? I know you have no reason to assist me, but it would devastate my remaining family—as small as they are—if they thought I killed somebody."

"Are you not able to dispose of it while you're healthy?" I asked.

"It is so difficult. Every time I pick it up, it reacts with fear. Despite the trouble I know it may cause me, I cannot bear to get rid of it."

"It appears to have been a while since you moved it."

"I regret to say that things have changed between us. I sit here most days in total silence."

Thomas's eyes dropped and he tilted his head. A less observant conversationalist would not have noticed the melancholy.

"I will do what I can to ensure that if you *are* suspected of murder, the police will learn that you only found the head, you didn't kill anybody." I assured him.

It was getting late, almost midnight in fact. I thanked him for his hospitality, and for being so open in describing his discovery. He thanked me for listening and for being a respectful guest. I told him I would tell nobody of his secret, unless necessary by the circumstances he had outlined. He was grateful.

I stepped out onto the front porch and the wind bit me like a hungry dog. On my way home I walked through the park, though it took a lot longer.

I didn't find anything interesting.

But One Day All of This Will be Gone

Alexander Zelenyj

In a world of despair and disappointment, one must continually rationalize and invent optimistic truths, when and where and however one can scrounge them, or risk suffocating beneath the inexorable weight of the everyday. Graspingly and achingly, naively and pathetically, and in the end—if fortune is with you—perhaps, even convincingly: this is the way by which we sometimes are able to save ourselves, however tenuously.

Bill Harliss considers this as he reads the crumpled letter in his hands with weary eyes, for what feels the millionth time, the individual words growing less meaningful with each subsequent reading, but the overarching bleakness of their message more profound than ever beneath the vulgar light filtering through the window. All the traffic light is blood red and morose, streetlight amber, pulsing upwards from the ground six floors below, with perhaps a melancholy influence of the moon's lingering light. He clutches the rolling pin in his other hand, its notched, wooden expanse glistening fiercely where he'd spent the better part of the past hour scrubbing away with the disinfectant soaked dish rag, hurting his fingers with the dedication of his efforts. He winces in examination of these haunted items, vision impaired by the gross swelling surrounding his left eye. His tongue probes cautiously along the interior of his battered, bloated bottom lip, tasting the metallic tang of blood, nudging a loosed tooth.

Eventually, he tears the paper into many pieces and lets these drift from his fingers, through the open window, and out onto the night air. He imagines their descent, twirling and graceful, deceivingly celebratory, like confetti in the pre-dawn gloom. He thinks of the night behind him and thinks of the year past, too. He ponders the people he has known, the stories of their

lives, and the nature of his intertwinement within them.
His is a deeply melancholic meditation: every memory,
every scenario is entwined with some deeply embedded
thread of misery.

He is weighted down with these ruminations, rooted
in his window-vantage chair, sweating in the sultry air,
baking beneath the suffocating trench coat wrapped
tightly about him like a cloak. Bill makes no move to
remove the heavy garment, nor turn on the rickety fan
standing silent sentinel nearby, among the detritus of his
belongings that congest the room. He is held immobile
by his thoughts, and only continues to ponder his life
and how he's come to this point—drunk, battered, and
alone in a cramped, mice-infested, non-air-conditioned
apartment, with the disparate pieces of his contentedness
drifting away into the night, unsalvageable, and a rolling
pin the weight of mountains resting across his lap.

He belches and can smell the lingering rot of rum,
which he's exhaled into the room. Several minutes pass
and, keeping the rolling pin across his lap, he removes
several crumpled papers from one of his coat pockets,
and a pen from the other. His hand grows possessed, and
attacks the papers with the pen. Tears well in his eyes,
muddying the work of his madly scribbling hand, but

still he writes and writes, without thought, impassioned, his heart speaking and urging him to record its Byzantine tale—desperately, frantically, fighting—as if seeking to arrive at some elusive truth in the unfolding text before him, or at the very least to save himself, however ephemerally, from the weight of the forthcoming day awakening outside.

Father's hands are dirtier and more frightening than nightmares…
But night can only last so long, and then a new day…

Your grandmother died in a hospital bed…
But you weren't close, and shed not a single tear.
Monty, with whom you were very close, died of a bum heart…
But milk bones were his favorite and you snuck him plenty.

13 always was the number that scared you…
But you were born the day following, and were thereby saved by a hair from ill omens.

Your girl's been seen in questionable and mysterious places…
But your first time in bed together remains vivid as photographic evidence.

The day job that you loathe is waiting at the end of a ten-year traffic jam…
But the universe of the car is electric with your most treasured song.

There are some businesses managed by dictators…
But your shift's done in less than ten.

Your husband hits the bottle, and then you…
But once, you saw a dinner plate-shape hovering like salvation in the clouds.

You watched your peers ditching together, relishing the days…
But hiding inside the library's study cubicle wasn't so bad—
you read books that took you farther away.
She took and she took, making you poorer than the destitute alley dweller…
But there was a time when she gave you fellatio with gusto, and regularly.

The band's '98 release was lackluster by their standards…
But 2000 proved a return to form, and a swelling of your proud heart: as a teenager music grew to define you, and gave you strength.

You regret the impulsive, foolish ink in your arm…
But watching movies in the dark allows you to pretend yourself clean.

He shouldered you clear and stared you down afterwards…
But fuck him—you're more intelligent than that cocksucker by far.

You loathe and fear this world of the crude and bellicose…
But who can tell what greater evils from which the Visigoths saved us?

The corners hold whores and the tenements house meth addicts…
But the world was once all jungle, and lizards roamed free of men: a thought by which to dream.

The blacks wore fetters and the Jews were cooked in ovens…
But rocket ships promised places above embarrassing histories.

*Rent is looming like thunderheads and student loans weigh
mountains...
But pitcher after pitcher brings brief periods of calm.*

*Turtles live longer than men...
But animals in captivity live statistically shorter lives.*

*This year's the same as last...
But tomorrow's your day off, who knows what may come?*

*You only cower through the streets of Detroit...
But your racist eyes were sculpted by American news
broadcasts over genetic predisposition.*

*He reminds you, when any opportunity arises, that he can kick
your ass—easy...
But you hate him better than anyone else could, ever.*

*The bus stop-milling high-schoolers turn insolent, challenging
you—the meek middle-aged loner—with looks...
But easy as anything, you pretend a bomb into the briefcase in
your hand.
Dad disappeared years ago...
But you gave him a birthday present once, when you were
little, and the two of you were still friends.*

*They never found the Devil who did it...
But in your dreams he burns every single night.*

*You saw an arm laying a hundred meters beyond the pile-up...
But you hadn't eaten breakfast that morning, and mostly water
came up.*

*You never did get to fuck your eighth grade teacher...
But dedication to fantasies has molded them into near-memory.*

You don't talk much these days...

But you used to walk the three hours home from the Mall together.

*The world might get to you through inflicting itself onto her...
But you can always seek vengeance on its every malign fold and sick crease.*

*He's a millionaire, and adored by many who know him little...
But you kicked his ass on the playground in seventh grade—a small, but great, victory you know he remembers.*

*He had his way and left her a laughing stock at the party...
But he pissed blood for some time, thereafter.*

*The taste of him haunts the back of your mouth...
But there are twenties in your pocket and the sun's setting on a long day, beaten at last.*

*She, the cruel queen to whom you'd stammered ineffectual adoration...
But she's due anytime now, and he's well on his way south.*

*You've fallen behind the pack in almost every way...
But if you stay indoors forever, who's to know?
Your friend dared you, and you couldn't summon the courage...
But the woman in question died of AIDs not three months past.*

*You can barely hold a decent barre chord...
But with eyes closed, you nightly conquer your bedroom stage.*

*You still feel somewhat awkward around her...
But at least she doesn't know what you made her do in your head that morning.*

The milk's turned into sewage and the cheese has grown a moldy beard...
But the disability check's in the mail and the liquor store closes at 10:00 tonight.

You'd rather die than work the line tomorrow...
But late night television awaits you at shift's end: something reliable besides the torture of the machines.

The post-work, late night talk shows and infomercials have begun to depress you, too...
But you own a book of Frank Frazetta paintings. Freedom-vistas opened for you, to roam un-squelched.

The dentist's chair—the terror today, as in childhood years of crooked teeth and a damaged social life...
But for now, there's a movie theatre and its safe, flickering-dark embrace.

Through the bedroom wall, you could hear dad pounding mom into the headboard at night...
But they hadn't been arguing, so you were eventually able to sleep.

He made you feel small in front of your friends...
But you might one night find him skunk-drunk and teetering in a lonely alley.

He treated all those women like meat and dirt...
But everyone knows now, and prison treats his kind in kind.

Your living quarters of one room and bath, and a laboring air conditioner, are oppressive with burning summer...
But winter always returns to murder the arrogant sun.

Your brother went to war and never returned...
But sometimes mystery means hope that closure would kill.

You failed again…
But one day, motherfuckers—one day.

You never did feel at ease there, among the suits and the ties…
But she locked the two of you in her office after the Christmas
staff party, yes she did.

You've lived another endless and angry day…
But you turned the arrogant trespasser spider into dust
beneath your heel.

Dad visited and, again, turned you ten years old …
But afterwards you beat the cat, and felt almighty once more.

You hear her crying next door every night…
But if you had her, you'd worship her like a goddess.

You dread your birthday year round…
But your romantic hope of vampires and fated nocturnal
encounters has never diminished.

They fucked up in overtime yet again…
But next year will be their year, and your season, too.

Christmas time is here again…
But they say most other people hate December, as well.

Father was the dragon, burning momma alive…
But maybe you'd become St. George if you prayed hard enough
for strength.

Another one's turned on you…
But tenacity is your virtue, if not one of many faults.

There are countless ways to make them all suffer…
But he's only got it in for their mother.

She's been with so many, so many since...
But you loved her truly, and felt like a mythological hero that
one entire year.

You understood, embarrassingly late, that he'd been
manipulating you...
But with you gone, he has no more puppets to make dance—
another man lonelier than you.

Brothers can be cruel that way...
But you filled his meals with secret, spiteful spit for years on
end.

Two white men mocked a third's skin, with words like knives,
while you said nothing...
But at least you refused to repeat the hateful teachings of your
father, ingrained in you like life lessons from an early age.

You emptied your stomach long into the post-party night and
morning...
But you felt the song in your gut, lingering like a thrumming
ghost all through your swooning seasickness.

You're stuck here forever...
But you once saw something strange and fiery arc across the
stars, headed upwards: you're a rare witness to something
freeing.

As a child, you felt misplaced most days after school ...
But the first person to learn about father's demonic persona
was your first girlfriend, when you were twenty-five and a
man in body, if not in courage.

You never thought you'd be like him...
But after the first time, in the first motel, with the first woman,
you regretted deeply your faithlessness.

It had been a true summer of pain for you…
But God helped you through it all, as the drunken wisdoms of
the sun-addled homeless woman, drinking mouthwash on the
street, had foreseen.

The one climbing into the pickup truck is no more than
fifteen…
But the driver might die the worst manner of death possible, for
his impending sin.

Father naming momma a fat whale and beaching her good all
over the bathroom floor…
But ancient peoples believed manatees to be mermaids,
beautiful, bewitching, and eternal.

You involuntarily recoiled as you passed the man of foreign
decent on the street…
But no one had noticed—you're still a good person.

Another mall kingdom glitters like a new jewel in the sun…
But somewhere, a sapling bends in the breeze.

Never a day devoid of dying armies…
But surely these things must end.

Trees, like men and women, fall all the time…
But many spring from a single seed.

The anchorman called the scene a nightmare…
But all manner of dreams must finally end.

You wanted her, yet she went with the enemy…
But you own many books and so have many friends to console
you.

The inclement sky again reflects your mood …

But your basement is deep and deep and deep.

Planes are dropping from the sky like flies these days…
But so are meteors, proof of movement beyond the clouds.

The lump inside your scrotum startled you, as you stood
beneath the shower's languorous mist…
But it might be nothing, nothing at all.

You fear the x-ray machine's illumination…
But you have a week of ignorance, within which to weigh
optimistic possibilities.

Hair thinner, eyes dimmer, while newly arrived cloud fronts
fog your brain…
But the average lifespan of males in your family gives you a
few more years, still.

True love never found you, and now all of a sudden you're
old…
But nobody has to know — you wear masks well enough.

You took advantage of a drunken girl once, years ago…
But you've nearly convinced yourself that she would have liked
it.

Your beloved puppy fell under car wheels late one summer
night…
But your friend's father died in a pile-up.

Four decades later and there may still be POWs caged in
Vietnam…
But you can read a less disheartening book of history instead.

A colonel once dreamed of peace between the settlers and the
tribes…

But dreams in which conflict is no longer a part of our genetic makeup, might one day come true.

The cops harass you and remain blind to teenage whores giving head in alleys...
But now you know to stay away from police, like you shun the criminal element, too.

You once caught a man filming you through the bathroom window...
But someone you know was raped behind a gas station one year ago.

The front page tells of a baby found dead in a garbage can...
But some babies grow to stalk and slay women.

The artist you admire, and call a hero, publicly mocked you...
But your memory was never very good—you forget disappointments as easily as victories.

Another child went missing from the neighborhood...
But maybe she's only dead.

He's better at everything than you ever will be...
But you could kill him if you really wanted.

Sleepless nights always prove the deadliest thinking time...
But you're certain there's a pill perfect for you.

The endangered species, black market, poaching ring skyrockets daily...
But there's another few thousand families fed.

The man in rags, asleep in the bus shelter, turns something in your belly...
But you've not fallen quite so far.

The mice in the walls remind you of just where you are today…
But the millions of broken-backed rodents you've trapped make you the king of this shitty, downtrodden empire.

You'd let both of them have you in quick succession…
But it's a secret, and a secret it will remain.

You deny the beggar's coin-questing hands…
But tell yourself that next time you'll pay for the escape in his bottle.

Your brother maintains that mother was unhappy on the day she died…
But he's been wrong about a great deal of important things.

A child died in the fire…
But you and your friends didn't think that anyone could be inside that ramshackle, derelict house.

The streets are cancerous, as diseased and perilous as the alleys…
But one might stumble upon unplumbed magic or miraculous science, smoldering among trash bins, if fortune is with them.

The dictator led his people through a reign of misery and woe…
But everyone lies wholly alone on their death bed.

His eyes had always unsettled you, alive with malignant fire…
But most disturbed individuals have histories of abuse.

The playground bully ruled your life with an iron fist and demented attention…
But you learned to love his relentless existence, when word got out that his father was in jail for molesting children.

A pair of cops getting blowjobs in the alley from a teenage boy...
But you'd needed a catalyst to become the lawgiver absent around you.

Your dreams are haunted by the boy incalculably older than his years...
But through these visions, you've been given strength to defy the waking world.

The city is teetering on the brink of ghetto-collapse...
But you'll retire where the lots are made of tall grass, sycamores, and wildflowers.

Guilt and guilt and guilt have grown like cancer behind your chest...
But you could have gone further with the sixteen-year old.

Shame owns you...
But heroes could wield worse weapons than kitchen utensils, for vanquishing the wicked and cruel.

You wake and find that all hope has been devoured by the new day...
But the dream from which you'd awakened seemed astoundingly real, and in it you'd flown.

True evil lives in the hearts of men...
But one day all of this will be gone.

But one day all of this will be gone.

A new beginning...

Bill Harliss—as if stirring from the deepest of slumbers—

turns his bloodshot, sleepless eyes from the ink-covered

paper to watch the awoken day outside the window. Full dawn startles him. The sun is a bloody warning, burning beyond the cityscape of buildings and rooftops in the east. The somnolent cooing of pigeons, lining the telephone wires, drifts on the air like some strange internal bodily noises of the buildings themselves. Cars squeal, brake, rev, and pass by beneath his apartment. A truck's horn barks like a gargantuan sea lion. The stink of exhaust, and rubber, and awakening humanity drifts to his nostrils and he breathes of it deeply, seeking the truth of it. This is his city, and the life that he has left.

He looks to his threadbare couch on the opposite side of the small room—purchased second-hand long ago— where he sleeps at night, forlorn-looking, unfriendly. The multitude of books bowing the shelves that line the opposite wall own a defeated look, their usual power to bolster his spirits, dormant. The brightening light frightens him, which crawls along his arms like a malignant presence that's bent on revealing him in every way for the man he is — small, and weak, and lonely, and living in an immense and cruel world of many (weak, when he should have been strong, on the threshold of utter defeat, when victory should have been his).

Yet, he'd lived through the night—he reasons—and that is something, something indeed. He places the wooden rolling pin onto the window sill, its immaculately shined surface flashing brilliantly in the sunlight. His numb hand feels the absence of its great weight. His other hand, also numb from its frenetic scratching at the papers, rests in his lap, circulation returning into its veins. He removes the papers from his lap and places them gently—nearly reverentially—upon the floor beside a crooked tower of books, newspapers, and family photo albums. He creaks forth from the skeletal wooden chair a moment later and makes his way to the couch, considers trying to befriend it in his quest for much-needed sleep and forgetfulness, and delicious escape inside of dreams untainted by knowledge of his every day.

He immediately realizes the futility of it. He would find no escape in sleep or dreams. He could never find solace in these old places again, for his pain ran too deeply, was too entrenched in the matrix of who he was—a great melancholy, born not only of his own experiences, but a collective sadness felt on behalf of every man and woman, boy and girl he'd ever known or been acquainted with, in even the most fleeting manner, everyone who shared a role in the aching, lonely, wicked and vengeful world he's come to fear and pity in equal measures, and which he's failed to save from its own fiery iniquity.

Bill Harliss unbuttons and shrugs the trench coat he's wearing to the apartment floor. The vivid, gay-colored latex costume is revealed: embarrassingly garish—he now sees—poppy-red and sunlight-yellow with baby-blue trim, his paunch making the material bulge blatantly, like a woman nearly due. This—his uniform and message of hope and strength to the city—is a failed proclamation, burning his cheeks more deeply than the stifling summer's oven-air could ever, a shamefully gaudy, generic symbol, like something culled thoughtlessly from pulp pages and brazenly seeking to be true. He spits onto the floor in self-loathing, grimaces with the pain the gesture awakens in his swollen, blood-encrusted lip. He senses something amiss inside his mouth, spits again, and watches entranced as his tooth clatters onto the floorboards like a pristine, blood-rooted jewel.

He turns and hastens across the small room in bold strides, which carry him to the window. He removes its tattered screen and drops it carelessly onto the floor.

Clambering onto the narrow, pigeon shit-encrusted window ledge, Bill steadies his body with a hand against the rough, brick façade of the tenement. The outdoors air is a relief on his skin, following the long night confined in the unventilated apartment, despite the oppressive heat. The chemical stink of the city is thicker outdoors. Along with the great height and the blinding sunlight, it dizzies him.

He draws himself erect, facing the brightening city— its countless buildings, and houses, and maze of streets zigzagging into the distance before him look especially ramshackle from his lofty vantage—with head held high. He raises a hand sunwards, thinking of feats attainable in dreams, prepared for flight.

Then—though, doubt overcomes him—he weeps anew. His sun-salute falters, and his hand falls trembling to his side. He blubbers through his tears, though he struggles to imbue the words with as much reserve and eloquence as he feels is deserved, if they indeed prove to be his epitaph: "I am your downtrodden dreams. I am your crushed, pissed-on hopes. I am occasional small victories, too. I am joy, and heartbreak, and contentedness, and shame, and sadness, and fury. I am Everyman. Maybe today is finally my day to find my happiness, and relief from all of this. I'm sorry to all of you whom I've hurt or disappointed in my time among you. I'm sorry I didn't have enough power, with which to protect you from the way of things. I've done what I could, and now I will try for you all one more time."

He boldly spikes his hands skywards and, as if answering his salute, the sun seems to brighten, intensifying the heat of its kiss into the bright skin of his costume. He edges another inch forward, until the tips of his bright cherry boots hang over the ragged, brick lip of the sill. His sunny cape flutters in a sudden surge of wind, beckoned upwards at its behest, as if impelling him to follow. Beneath him—six stories far, far below— the hazy city has fully awoken into the new burning day, and begun its great and furious, and ravenous clamor.

Rapture
S. MacLeod

Wisps of silver-like string float, central, above Ben as he
speaks. Glasses glint under fluorescents, silver string
waves—slight current. He's saying something about
God's love. It's nothing I haven't heard before.
Earnestness in the place of reason, or quantitative
method, makes me tired.

Shift, wince as the bandages stick against the mess
I've made. No one's offering sympathy—it's my third
time at this. The first time, the ER doctor turned green,
patched me up, and sent me home. The second time, she
turned white. I spent two weeks in Psych with the other
patients, who were like dark blooms with teeth, fragile

and scary. Programs and groups, and all I really learned was how *not* crazy I am. Their silver strings, short and frayed, existent but damaged.

"God loves you, you know," Ben says, takes off his glasses, runs a hand over his face.

I'm tempted to put a hand on his knee, a game I play because he's a homophobe (worse, one in denial of his own homophobia), but the effort isn't worth the reward. I shouldn't be so mean—he's trying, and he's here. No one else could be bothered, certainly not dear Mother.

The God speech is the same old, so I lie back, watch Ben's silver string curl gently as he speaks, dips his head, moves his hands. If God is infinite, and my whole existence is less than a speck on an atom, how would God even notice? They're pointless, circular arguments. My lower back is sore from the position I'm in on the hospital bed. Shift, again wince.

"Sometimes, it's just not enough," I point out, timed barb, well sharpened from years of use. "If what you people say is true, God is up there," point at the ceiling, somewhere in the acoustic tile maybe, "and that's no good to me down here."

Still and silent, he's watching me. I try to not notice how attractive he is—in a hipster kind of way—with his shaggy hair and secondhand clothes. I want to use the washroom, but don't want him to see. It's silly, I know, but I want to be spared *some* of what dignity it is I have left.

"Hey, would you do me a favor?"

Ben looks relieved.

"There's a machine down the hall, would you grab me a cup of ice, please?"

As soon as he's gone, I swing my legs over the side of the bed and bend double at the burning pain of it. This is the part I forget when I'm in the moment, the stretching and itching as the cuts heal, the way that fabric sticks and sweat slips in, salt-sharp. I creep toward the bathroom, trying to keep covered, even though the other men in the ward don't care, sunk into their own pain. Their strings are frayed, short wicks like burnt-out candles.

In the washroom, I lift the hospital gown out of the way. The other times I did this the weals were deep gashes, the scabs black-red and the outer skin pink, and hot with infection. That's part of the ritual, pry the scabs back—the deeper the better—pull a safety pin through green goo, then pour peroxide and watch it bubble. These new cuts are covered in rough-soft bandages and surgical tape.

How to explain what it's really like to loathe this blameless flesh? How the only way to sever the feedback loop of fear and anxiety is to slice through it with something sharp? It's a cold comfort, knowing these wounds will heal no matter how much I pick at them.

I can't get at what I really want to carve out of myself.

Turn on the tap, stream cool water in the steel sink basin, splash my face. I try not to look in the mirror, hating the sight of my watery brown wall-eyes and receding hair line, sunken chest and scarecrow arms. The hospital soap is pink, antiseptic. Carefully wash each digit on my hands—the nails, the wrists, some imagined grime in the bracelets of fortune—I don't want to track back any nastiness for the hospital staff to catch.

Think about…stabbing my leg and tearing out the nerves in a long string, like tangled Christmas lights. They only give me a painkiller at night, and I'm not sure they know what to do with me.

I'm rearranging the covers, when Ben returns with a large Styrofoam cup of ice. He sets it down on the table, but remains standing in front of the chair. My bed is closest to the door and I can see past him into the hallway, see rolling carts and part of the nurses' station.

He apologizes for taking so long. "When are you

getting out?" he asks.

"Probably tomorrow. They only admitted me because I lost too much blood."

He nods and then looks at me. He doesn't speak, seems to be studying me, and I resist the urge to pull the blankets up over my head.

"Why don't you come to church with me on Sunday — if you can?"

I chew on my lip. He's invited me before, and I went a couple of times.

"Look, Ben, your church friends are really nice and all, but it's just not my scene. I'm really not comfortable around them."

"If you'd just give it a chance," he starts.

"I have. I've bent over backwards to find out about your faith, and I've met your friends. In case you haven't noticed, none of them like me."

"That's not true. They all like you."

"Look, I wouldn't drag you anywhere you weren't comfortable. How about you come to a fetish party with me? How would you feel trying to make small talk with, say, Caitlynn, wearing nothing but a pair of leather pants and some electrical tape?"

His eyes widen, pious pistons work overtime in his

brain. I'm not sure if the image scares him or turns him on—probably both. Caitlynn is his friend Ted's wife.

"Besides, my mother was a Pentecostal Christian. No offense to you or your family, but I got enough of that growing up."

Including the time she caught me masturbating and pulled me into the living room by the ear, forced me to read the Bible with my pants around my ankles, and then slammed the Good Book on my penis a few times for good measure. It didn't hurt that much, but the burning shame of it, the way she flicked my scrotum with her fingers the way you'd try to get rid of a stuck speck of dirt, and the sound of the paper, flapping like dusty wings.

I blink back sudden tears, not wanting Ben to see.

After another twenty minutes of awkward small talk, Ben leaves and I turn off the light over my bed. It's not late, but I'm tired. He means well, I tell myself, but he always gives me the feeling that I've failed somewhere. The conversation has ground me down.

The word grind, grinding, to grind—ground—I imagine sticking my dick in one of those school pencil sharpeners, turning the handle, and watching the skin peel away in a spiral, a small, bloody flesh cone. Scoop out my eyes with a melon baller, the kind that has a serrated edge and a wooden handle.

I rub the heel of my hand against my thigh, and find a small scarred patch of skin that's not bandaged. Rubbing it does nothing to settle my jittery stomach and jumpy head. The other men in the ward snore gently, like small animals. Night sounds the chirps and beeps of mechanical birds.

*   *   *

Home now, bang the door shut three times—until it latches the right way—go to the stove, to be sure I didn't leave it on. Check my cell phone—there's a message from my boss. I shut the phone off and toss it in the nightstand. Mother hates that I never answer my phone, but if I want to talk to anyone, I'll call them. I loathe cell phones, mostly use mine to play Pac Man or Space Invaders — tiny versions of the games I liked as a kid, with better graphics.

My one room bachelor place smells musty and unused, even though I've only been away for two nights. I open a window, lie carefully on my back, on my mattress on the floor. The sheets are stained with brownish stripes of dried blood, dead copies of the cuts on my stomach and thighs. I should really get clean ones, but I can't be bothered.

The sounds of summer in the neighborhood filter in—heavy traffic, birds trilling, and the occasional dog bark. When I feel okay on my days off, I sometimes like to walk around at night. Other times I stay inside until the walls breathe, and want to pound my fists against panel-covered cinder block, feel the sides of my wrists bruise and buckle.

I put a pillow under my head and look down at my chest, wonder what it would be like to have a silver string. That's my secret—I don't have one and don't know how to explain my conclusions to Ben. When I'm on my own, it's okay, but being around people reminds me of how removed I am from them. It's the same reason most of my relationships fail. I've been told I'm just afraid to love, or I'm in denial, or in the closet—none of which is true. Sometimes, I wonder what would happen if I really told the truth, broken open like when you get a light bulb wet—*fission*.

The silver strings first appeared to me, interestingly enough, during a church service. I did try to see things

Ben's way, my mother's way, because it's like they always have a backup plan. Somehow, God's love is enough, even when the world is crumbling. My mother could be sitting on the broken ruins of everything and she'd be rocking back and forth, cuddling her Bible. After years and years of darkness, I wondered what it would be like to be in the light.

The church meetings were okay. I liked the friendliness of it, that's something I never found in any other so-called community. They'd actually walk up, say hello, and tell you their names. They're nice enough people, but underneath there's this dialogue, this "I'm a Christian and you're not—so, you're going to burn in hell".

I stopped going because I got tired of feeling judged. Something slithers under their Sunday suits, something I don't trust. At least I acknowledge the black holes in my soul. They step over their soul-holes like they're not there (at least, I used to think that—until I started seeing the silver strings). Maybe, they do have something I don't.

It was after the first part of the sermon, during the "prayer". Instead of closing my eyes and thinking about something else, or flipping through the hymnal, I took a look around. The lights in the room dimmed and I could

see, above everyone, all these wispy silver strings, like
the tethers in a balloon bouquet. Each string started over
its owner's heart, and it was like the room was an x-ray
or a negative of itself. The people were vague shapes,
except for a light over their hearts and a string that
snaked through the seventh chakra and out the tops of
their heads, and up, and up, and up. I had a vision of the
whole world as a negative. These silver strings all twined
together, out into the macro verse, out to what God really
is—a pulsing, twinkling sphere of energy made up of
strings. In my excitement, I looked into my own heart.

I didn't have a string, just a spot of darkness. The dim
heat of bloodletting is the only warmth I feel, alone with
my scars, and secrets, and shame.

I yank the bandages off and rub my hands over the
burning batch of cuts, the dry ridges under my fingers
that have yet to grow into the skin. They don't belong,
but they will.

*   *   *

After breakfast, I turn my phone back on and call my
manager. I'm standing in my kitchenette, one hand on

the counter, a headache clusters behind my eyes. I can feel it waiting to spring into a migraine.

"Hi, Sheila."

She greets me, then there's an awkward pause. I ask for my hours.

"Look, um…" Pause again.

My stomach starts to twist—a windsock, a DNA helix, two slugs fucking on a stem.

"I don't think this is working out." Sheila sounds apologetic.

I lean against the counter and wipe my hand over my face. "So, I'm fired."

"I'm really sorry, but we can't keep someone who's so…"

"Crazy."

"Unreliable. But now that you mention it, maybe you should try welfare or disability. I'm sure the province has programs that can help you…"

I hang up on her and lean over the sink. The spot of darkness in my chest rises in noxious waves. I dry heave, choking on my meal until it finally comes up in a glut of eggs and toast. The pain behind my eyes settles into a heavy thud.

After I clean up, I find my tools and heavy elastics,

hunch my shoulders against flying, black attacking things—things in the shadows, smoke and arrows—run my hands over my hair, down my shoulders and arms, scritch-scratch. This time I'm going through with it. Maybe, if I cut off the hormonal flow, things will be better—calmer. I tried making new skin entirely of scars, and it didn't help, so eliminating the damned thing will.

First, the ritual—douse in alcohol and run cleansing fire over every blade. I'm not taking chances on infection, so I change my mind and boil everything. Lay it out in a steel pan: X-Acto knife, sluice-sharp and precise, heavy rubber bands, and black electrical tape still in its package. I can't sterilize that or the bands, so I'll have to make do. Then, I lay out the scary-looking tool. The veterinary supply store didn't ask questions. I wish for a second I had some help with this.

Sterile gloves in their little package and a dressing supply tray I took from my mom's ages ago. I take my clothes off and change the sheets. I take my work items over to the bed, and then make a wrap of ice cubes in a wet washcloth, a bowl of ice within reach. I sit on the mattress, use a mirror, try to find a comfortable position—legs up and bent in the middle like a soft sculpture.

When I'm ready, I peel back the top of the supply tray, and then use the little tongs and a bandage pad to swab my hairless groin with rubbing alcohol. It stings. The newest cuts are crusted, already healing. The stitches ladder their way up both thighs. What's left of my penis is flayed, flesh butterfly wings, with a small opening to urinate. The small silver rings that separated the flesh are gone, lost somewhere in the operating room. The balls are mostly intact, though pink and scarred from torture sessions. Scarred flesh feels less. I was trying for a new skin, of my own creation, but now I won't need it.

I take heavy elastic, and tightly twist it around the base of my left testicle, then repeat for the right. I do this once more, then the same with the electrical tape, and around the scrotum—tight, tight, tight, like Mother said—until the flesh is hard and red. The pressure builds in a dull ache, slow and bright like sunset, so I pop four of the painkillers they prescribed. I have to go easy on them, for they're in short supply—stingy doctors. As if a pill addiction would not be the least of my worries. I wash the welcomed, white pills down with a bottle of water from the floor beside me.

After an hour, the flesh turns from red to a deep purple. I apply the ice wrap, and the pain subsides from a sharp current to a duller, deeper throb.

"Is this what they call blue balls?" I say out loud. Laughter feels good, snowflakes that melt in my mouth.

The tool looks like a large pair of pliers with a circle in the middle, closed at the top to pinch, hard and heavy for workhorses and solid-footed oxen. I take a deep breath and apply it up under the balls, steel pressure on the scrotum.

"A man goes to a rub and tug, has a great time, but gets some kind of infection." I'm aware this is whistling in the dark, or something. I press, bear down—o, god the pressure.

"A few days later, his penis turns yellow, then green—*oh, oh*. In a panic…*huh*…he goes to the doctor. *Hoo*. Doctor says, 'I'm sorry sir, uh…we're going to have to amputate.' *Ah huh*.

"Man says, 'No thanks' and goes to another doctor, then to an urologist. *Ohhhh…*

"They all say the same—*huh*—thing. Finally, he breaks down and goes to a doctor specializing in Chinese medicine. 'Do you have to amputate?' the man asks.

"'No, no,' the doctor says.

"'Oh thank god,' man says. *Eeeeee…*

"'No, another day or two, that thing gonna fall off by

itself.' *Ahh huh…"*

My voice is down to a croak, and I no longer feel like laughing. I try to press harder on the tool, but I'm not strong enough and the crushing sensation makes me sick to my stomach, green and sour. The world tilts, dark things close in, and I lean over hoping I don't throw up into my tool tray. After a few minutes, the nausea subsides. I release the tool and toss it into the tray.

I stand up to go pee, again having to wash and rub down the work area. The pills make me tired, so I settle back and try to nap. It's hard to find a comfortable position. Trying to lie on my stomach or my side is impossible, so I put a pillow behind my back and it's a little better.

I try to imagine the new me—more confident, a spring in my step. This really does make me laugh. Laughing sends fresh twists of agony through my groin, deeper green shot through with black. I try to read a book, to concentrate on something other than the pain. Someone once asked me why, and I told them: Scars are the marks of the wars a man's been through, battles he's won.

After six hours, I'm weeping. I hold off on the pills, and then take two more when I can't stand it. After twelve hours, it's all I can do to not shriek. I'm covered in sweat, curling and uncurling my legs, the bed beneath me soaked. I take two more pills, and I only have a few left. Even the ice cubes I packed underneath me didn't do anything to numb the nerves. They've all melted, leaving a wide wet patch.

All the previous pain I've felt in the world was a rehearsal compared to this, including the furious, twisting burn of a dislocated shoulder, when Mother pushed me down the stairs.

Fifteen hours and I'm on my knees, pressing my sweaty face into the pillow. I want to shove my hands between my legs, anything to take away the pressure, but if I do I'll get an infection. My hands flap against my thighs like injured pigeons.

"That's what you get for being dirty," mother's voice in my mouth. I can smell her perfume—Cabochard, because she said it was something that rich ladies wore. I fucking hate Cabochard. I wipe the back of my hand across my mouth, bat at something I see just out the corner of my eye.

There are coyotes on the Canamera Parkway.

Aaaahooooo, long howl—*huh, huh, huh*. Scrabble around on the mattress, until I can see out the window.

The clouds bruise up across the sky. Tomorrow it will be a full moon.

My body, my soul, God, the devil—something takes mercy on me at the eighteen-hour mark. The light in the room darkens from early morning grey to welcome black.

When I wake up the room is dark. My mouth is dry and I need to pee. Without thinking, I swing both legs around to the side of the mattress, and lightning bolts of pain shoot through me. I put my hands out flat to steady myself, breathe deep until it subsides. Haul myself up, carefully, until I can stand. With one hand over my groin, and my water bottle in the other, I make my way to the bathroom. I haven't eaten in two days, my stomach's a stone. Flush, clean up with rubbing alcohol, and I fill the bottle at the tap.

Back on the mattress, I turn on a light and check the progress. After the initial shock of movement, the pain has subsided to a dull ache no worse than a tooth abscess. Calm steals over me, the way a sunrise feathers its way into morning clouds. I drink small sips of water. My balls are hard black eggs, lifeless and cool to the touch. Hours pass, my thoughts are blank and still as a standing pool.

*   *   *

After a couple of days in bed, I'm again ready to try the tool. I take the outer layer of black tape off and clean the area with alcohol, leaving the elastics. My X-Acto knife is ready for the final stage of the operation—if needed. I swallow the last six pills in the bottle, wishing I'd held onto a few. There's a bottle of whiskey in the cupboard if it comes to that, but I don't think it will.

I again take the tool out, feel the weight of the blades. Using a mirror, I line the blades up, and bring my thighs together for extra support. I take a deep breath—one, two, three—and bring the blades together as fast and hard as I can. The pain comes rushing back into flesh I thought was dead, black-red crushing, pulling agony, and the world goes dark.

I wake up in the fetal position, the tool still clamped around the lifeless flesh of my balls. Sweat greases my back and scalp. Groan. Roll. I Sit up, draw my legs closer. The X-Acto knife is within easy reach, still in the bowl of sterilized instruments. I have to do this quick, before I pass out.

I lift the mirror, but can't see much. Going by feel, I slice the X-Acto knife in a fluid, circular motion. It's like trying to saw through thick foam rubber, but the blade is the sharpest one I have, so it will have to do.

I once tried to cut my leg with a butcher knife. My skin stretched open in a wide white trough, red spots welled into drops that joined and ran streaks, skin stripes.

Hack through the layers, and pry back pulpy, purple, blackened, ruined flesh, the pain deep and white. I hold my breath against a putrid smell, like organ meats gone over. My body no longer belongs to me. It's a job to be finished. My mouth sets in a sneer. This is good, this is clean. I cut and pull it back, the sooner it's gone the better. There is no blood, the vessels closed off and dead days ago.

Finally, what's left of my balls, hang by a flap of skin. I clench my teeth and feel a growl grow in my throat, as I attack the last stubborn, leathery piece. It separates at last, and I rip the hated sac away from my body, drop it in the tray. Disengage the tool.

Relief rushes through me, and something else. I look down at the ragged ends of flesh, black and green like night fungus. As I stare, I'm sure I can see tiny silver lights start to spark.

I open my heart and feel the string alight, alive, course through my chest on its way out the top of my head, and up, and up, and up.

The Writers

Dakota Taylor is a freelancer and student. He is a member of the writing workshop litreactor.com and lives in Phoenix, Arizona.

Alan Wor is a 24 year-old college dropout. Before he quit, he was studying for a BFA in Fiction. He was about halfway there. Now he works in a little liquor store in a little town. He is heading where he is heading, about as fast as anyone else. His short stories and poetry have been published in the *Kokanee, Not About Religion*, and the *Tahoe Blues* anthology.

Byron Alexander Campbell thinks and writes in all sorts of weird spaces, liminal spaces, spaces that should not or do not exist. An MFA degree candidate at the California Institute of the Arts, he is currently at work on an ergodic novel. Find out more at theyearisyesterday.wordpress.com.

Ralph Robert Moore's latest short story collection, *I Smell Blood*, can be ordered from a number of venues by going to: ralphrobertmoore.com/books.html. In The Short Review AJ Kirby said, "*I Smell Blood*, Ralph Robert Moore's second short fiction collection, reinforces his reputation, amongst those in the know, that here we have a genre-storytelling giant in our midst…this is a surefire cult hit which deserves wider recognition."

Dave Fragments retired to the countryside of Western Pennsylvania amidst the deer and squirrels to write short stories and an occasional poem. He has published Spec. Fiction, Horror, and Poetry in online publications and anthologies. For many years he did research into coal liquefaction and heterogeneous catalysis.

Eric Pollarine is an author and freelance writer, who lives, works, writes, smokes, never sleeps, and drinks far too much coffee in Cleveland, Ohio. His short fiction can be seen around the web and in print. His first novel *This Is The End*, is available through Amazon.

Nicky Peacock is an English author in the UK. Further information on her and her work can be found at: http://www.creativemindswriting.co.uk/page18.htm and http://www.librarything.com/profile/Nicky-Peacock

Jared Donald Blair lives in Marysville, Washington, where he works, plays music, writes stories, and watches horror movies. He is interested in medical oddities and professional wrestling, and believes that horror is about monsters, but also—more importantly— about how people react to those monsters. Jared is currently working on a novel about childhood, ghosts, overly friendly neighbors, Bigfoot, and what's buried in peoples' backyards.

Abram S. Jacobs lives in western Massachusetts. He is a former intelligence reporter for the U.S. Air Force, and a former letter carrier with the U.S. Postal Service. He enjoys hiking in the forest. His real name is LYAFETTUV (a simple cipher).

Todor Oluic was born and raised in Windsor, Ontario and has been writing since before birth. His first manuscript was written in utero, but was shelved for being too "topical". This is his first published piece.

Leonora Stein is a book junkie and pusher. She owns Babbo's Books in Brooklyn, NY. She's a compulsive nail-biter and thinks about death way too much—any amount is too much. She has a story in Curbside Splendor, Issue 3.

Scott Barbour is a writer and editor from San Diego. He is a member and volunteer for San Diego Writers, Ink, a nonprofit organization that promotes writing and appreciation of the literary arts. His work has appeared in A Year in Ink, Volumes 3, 4, and 5 (Ink Spot Press).

Jess Gulbranson is the author of novels *10 A BOOT STOMPING 20 A HUMAN FACE 30 GOTO 10*, *Mel*, and *Antipaladin Blues*. His short fiction, poetry, and art have been featured in Lambshead's Cabinet of Curiosities, Kizuna, Umbrella Journal, and Bradley Sands Is A Dick. For Crappy Indie Music: The Blog he is a critic, interviewer, and douchebag-in-residence. Living in Portland, Oregon with his wife and daughter, Gulbranson also makes music under the names Coeur Machant and DJFalsifier.

William Cook is a writer/illustrator from NZ and a member of the Australian Horror Writers Association. Previously published in Canta, Zephyr, Poetry NZ(20), Southern Ocean Review, Side Stream, Indite Circle & Blackmail Press (20). Short stories published in Remark (USA) issue 34 June '05 and Mindfire Renewed June '05. 'Devil Inside' published in Masters of Horror Anthology 2010. Cover artist/contributor for Putrid Poetry & Sickening Sketches 2011. Debut novel: 'Blood Related,' published by Angelic Knight Press December 2011.

Sam D. Church II graduated from the University of Alberta's Secondary Education program. His prose and poetry have been published in several journals, including Burner Magazine, Toucan, and Touch Poetry. He currently resides in London, England.

M.J. Nicholls is a firm believer in the brief bio. He lives in Edinburgh and writes fiction and its opposite

Cornelius Fortune is an award-winning journalist, whose work has appeared in The Advocate, Metro Times, Chess Life, Yahoo News, Novel & Short Story Writer's Market, Tales of the Unanticipated, Illumen and others. Fortune has written extensively on popular culture, comic books and 21st century trends. He is also a Rhysling nominated poet and the author of Stories from Arlington. In addition to journalism, he mostly writes poetry and less-than-interesting grocery lists, devoid of imagery or clever alliteration. Visit his website at www.corneliusfortune.com or his blog, "Pop Culture Saturation," at http://corneliusfortune.blogspot.com.

James Beaton lives in Toronto, Canada with his two black cats. He enjoys the macabre and writes humor, horror, and dark fiction with psychological tension. He has published short stories and has some forthcoming.

Alexander Zelenyj is the author of the books Experiments At 3 Billion A.M., Black Sunshine, and the forthcoming short fiction collection, Songs For The Lost. His fiction has appeared in many publications, including Revelation, Euphony, Inscape, Front & Centre, Freefall, Blind Swimmer, Way Out West, Columbia And Britannia, Sex And Murder, Pulp Empire, Structo, Underground Voices, and The Medulla Review. He lives on the 6th floor in Windsor, Ontario, Canada. His online home—also on the 6th floor—can be found at www.alexanderzelenyj.com.

S. MacLeod holds a BA in Communications and works nights, where she talks to strange people and has lots of time to dream about weird things. Her work has appeared in Nepenthe (Wilfrid Laurier University's poetry journal) and the e-zine Luna Station Quarterly, and has been accepted for upcoming publications from Twisted Library Press and Static Movement.

Original Cover Sketch
by
Anthony Noel

www.ingramcontent.com/pod-product-compliance
Lightning Source LLC
Chambersburg PA
CBHW051233260626
47162CB00002B/401